HERE, THERE BE DEMONS

FROM THE CHRONICLE OF PIP OF PANDARA

CHARLES RAY

North Potomac, MD

For information about this and other works of this author, contact the author at charlesray.author@yahoo.com.

Cover art and design by the author.

Author photo by Denise Ray-Wickersham

Printed in the United States of America.

ISBN: 0692600841
ISBN-13: 978-0692600849

Dedication

This book is dedicated to fantasy fans; those who believe ogres, fairies and trolls actually exist out there somewhere, and that dragons exist and can fly.

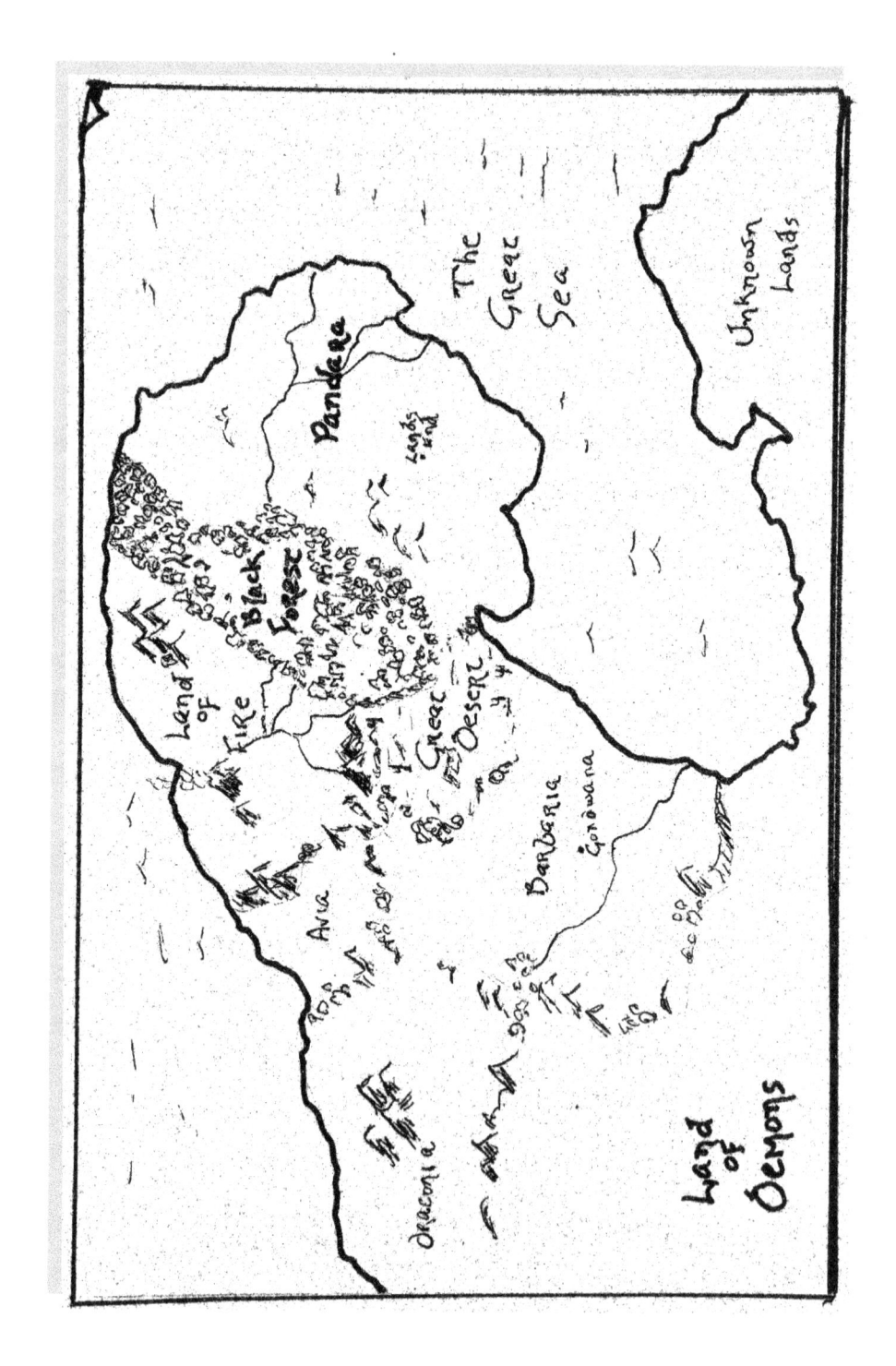

ONE

Pip sat at the large wooden desk, staring down at the pile of documents overflowing its top. He shook his head, and then bowed it, cupping his hands to either side, fingers entwined in his flame red hair.

"This is not how it was supposed to be," he said to himself. "A soldier is not supposed to have to battle stacks of paper."

Through slitted eyes he stared down at the unruly parchments piled there, silently swearing that they seemed to have grown in number in the few minutes he'd been staring at them. There were supply requests from the quartermaster's office with Tamara's untidy scrawl at the bottom of each. Tamara, a fairy of wood and water, did double duty as chief of the quartermaster unit and chief trainer for scouting and reconnaissance. It was the second duty that she much preferred, but her ability with figures had forced Pip to give her the additional duty of keeping track of the many supplies needed to keep his small army feed, clothed and equipped. The volume of requests from her office, though, was her way of getting back at him for the odious office duty which she hated, a fact that she reminded him of each time they met. Beneath that was a smaller pile of documents, mainly from his two regimental commanders, Godfred and Melchor, informing him of their training schedules, plans for recruitment to fill the ranks, and notifications of disciplinary actions—thankfully, there were only a few of these—mostly for minor infractions.

That each of his subordinate chiefs felt it necessary for him to see so much paper was for Pip a constant source of frustration.

What he really ached to do was be out in the field, working with the still green soldiers of Pandara's national army. No, he reminded himself; fully a third of the ranks were filled by beings from the Land of Fire, making it a combined Pandaran-Land of Fire force. He had yet to think of an appropriate name, so everyone kept the name, National Army of Pandara, shortened to NAP by the soldiers and officers alike. That name would have to go, he thought. He did not want to lead a force called NAP, it sounded too much like a band of vacationers whose aim was to find a place to . .

. take a nap. But, try as he might, he'd been unable to think of a more suitable designation.

He felt the beginning of a headache, a dull throbbing at his temples that always came when he wrestled with naming the army. *Oh well, that'll have to be a task for another day.* He took the quill pen from its ivory holder, dipped it in the inkwell until the tip was black, and quickly scribbled his name at the bottom of each document. When he'd signed the final document, he stacked them neatly to the left side of his desk. After putting the pen back in its holder, he leaned back and sighed deeply.

A few moments later he sat upright. "Norbert," he called. "Norbert."

His aide-de-camp, Norbert, rushed into the office.

"Yes, your highness," he said. "What do you require?"

Pip looked up at the young soldier. The gold star on his collar, signifying his recent promotion to lieutenant, reflected the light from the lamp on Pip's desk.

"What I require, Norbert, is for you to call me commander, not your highness. We are in the army here, not the throne room. Here I am the commander."

"B-but, your high-, er commander, you are the heir to the throne, second only to her majesty, Queen Daphne. It hardly seems appropriate for me not to--"

Pip waved his hand in a choppy motion, causing the young man to stop mid-sentence with his mouth hanging open.

"That is an order, *Lieutenant*. We will follow military discipline in this army. Am I clear?"

Norbert's back straightened and he threw his shoulders back.

"Aye, sir, commander, sir," he said.

"Good," Pip said. He smiled. "Now, I want you to take this forsaken paperwork from my desk and return it to the authors. I am going to my quarters to have a few words with Lady Zohra, and after that you and I will go on an inspection of the army, so get our horses ready."

"Aye, commander." Norbert beamed a broad smile as he gathered the papers. "Should I bring the mounts to your quarters?"

"No, I'll meet you at the stables."

Norbert clicked his heels and bowed his head slightly. Pip would have preferred a salute, but the man was holding the documents against his chest with both hands.

"Aye, commander, I will wait for you at the stable."

Pip rose as Norbert marched smartly out. He could not restrain a smile, thinking that young Norbert just a short time before had been a farm boy, new to the army, when Pip had taken him on the mission against the evil tyrant Tenkuk in Barbaria. The lad had acquitted himself well in that operation, and upon his return, Pip had made him his aide, recently promoting him to a rank befitting the aide-de-camp of the army commander.

Pip adjusted his tunic as he walked toward the door. At the door, he took his sword from the rack and belted it around his waist. Chuckling, he exited his office. Zohra, he knew, would chide him for wearing it when he visited her in her chambers, but he didn't want to take the time to return to his office for it before joining Norbert at the stable.

As he'd guessed, his wife's eyes went directly to the sword at his waist when he entered the bedchamber.

"So, now that I'm heavy with child, my husband finds it necessary to arm himself before approaching me," she said wryly. "Am I truly that unattractive?"

Pip pulled up short, his mouth agape. For a few heartbeats he was at a loss for words. Unattractive? His Zohra? Far from it. He'd found that as her belly grew rounder with the life she carried inside her body, she seemed to become radiant, that he desired her even more. When he gazed upon her face, his breathing stopped, and his heart beat so fiercely he feared it would burst from his chest.

"No, my dearest wife," he said when he could at last find his voice. "You are without doubt the most beautiful woman in all of Pandara; nay, the most beautiful in the entire known and unknown universe."

Zohra, now in her sixth month of pregnancy, lowered her gaze. Her cheeks darkened. She could not stifle the smile that turned her carmine lips upward. But, Zohra of Avia, of the

Eagle Clan, was not one to let her victim off easily.

"If I am truly such a beauty, then why do you find it necessary to wear your sword in my presence?"

Pip looked closely. He saw the twitching of her lips, and knew that she was having her amusement with him. He let out the breath that he'd been holding. Since she became pregnant, Zohra had been subject to many swings of mood, she desired many strange and exotic foods, and at times could not hold food in her stomach, especially in the early mornings. He could never know when her words were in jest or the signal for an angry outburst of recrimination or tears. Truly, he thought, what a child did to a woman's body and mind was amazing—and quite frightening. At least now, though, she seemed to be in a playful mood.

"I am on my way to the stable," he said. "I am riding with Norbert out to inspect the regiments at training outside the city. It would have been out of my way to have to return to my office for my sword. Please forgive me, my dear, for bringing it into your bedchamber."

Zohra put her hands over her mouth. Her body shook. Then, she burst out laughing.

"Truly, Pip," she said between gasps of laughter. "You are far too easy. You know I do not mind. In fact, I would like very much to ride with you. Being confined to this castle is driving me mad."

That Pip could easily understand. Zohra had

been one of her tribe's most fearless warriors, spending much of her day on horseback patrolling the boundaries of their land and fighting off bandits and predators. Since learning of her impending motherhood, however, Queen Daphne had, through the castle physician, ordered that she remain within the confines of the structure, lest some misfortune befall the child she carried—a child that would fall just behind Pip himself as heir to the crown that the good Queen Daphne, Pip's aunt, wore.

"I know how you feel, goodwife," he said. "But, we can take no chances of harm coming to our son."

"Or, daughter, good husband." She put the cloth she'd been embroidering down on the table at her knees and smiled up at him. "You know there is as much chance of the child being a girl as a boy, given the numbers of girls born to my people, more in fact."

She slapped the table, hard enough to make it jump, and cause Pip to flinch.

"Oh, pshaw," she said. "Women of the Eagle Clan often ride until just days before delivering their young. You Pandarans treat women as if they were some fragile piece of tableware."

Pip wanted to argue the point, but he knew two things; one was that arguing with Zohra was like trying to hold back the flow of a river with a spoon, and two, she had made a valid point. The women of Pandara, other than those who worked beside their men on the farms outside the capital, were not at all accustomed to labor more strenuous than sweeping a dusty house or washing a pot of dirty laundry. He also knew that he loved the dusky young Avian, who, even with her swollen belly, was the most beautiful creature he'd ever laid eyes on.

"I-I will talk to the queen," he said. "Mayhap she will agree that if you are in a carriage, it would be possible for you to get outside the castle from time to time."

A hopeful expression brightened Zohra's face. "Oh, Pip, my darling, if you could do that I would be ever so happy. I have never been forced to spend so much time inside before."

She picked the cloth up, holding it up and studied it closely.

"So, this trip of yours . . . how long will it take?" she asked, cocking her head to the side and eying him, reminding Pip of the bird for which her clan was named.

"I think mayhap two . . . three days . . . not more."

Her face fell. Pip felt his heart sink within his chest. Since the wedding he'd not spent a night away from her. Now, he knew, no matter how strong she might be, how valiant a warrior, she needed him at her side. But, he needed to get away from the confines of his small office for a few days or he would go mad.

Zohra's gaze softened. She smiled. It was a small smile, with more than a hint of sadness, but the expression in her eyes told Pip that she understood.

"Very well, Pip," she said in a quiet voice. "Ride safely and return soon."

She stood as Pip crossed the space between them. His arms encircled her shoulders and she pressed her face against his chest, wrapping her arms around his waist and pulling him close. He held her thusly for a long time, breathing in the fragrance of the scented soap she'd taken to using to wash her flowing black hair; a soap that smelled of a field of sweet flowers. The warmth of her body could be felt through the leather vest he wore over the blue silk tunic.

Mayhap two days will be enough. I will surely miss her sorely after only one.

Charles Ray

TWO

Even Nightshade, Pip's steed since his visit to the Land of Fire, was happy to be leaving the confines of the city. Once they passed the last shop and entered the open countryside, the black stallion got a peppier stride in his step and flung his head back and forth, whipping his mane against Pip's hands.

Pip could see when he glanced back at his aide-de-camp, that even Norbert, riding to Pip's left and slightly behind, with a pack horse carrying their tents and equipment behind him, was also smiling broadly. He, too, was happy to get outside the city.

While the countryside, especially that area of farms that lay to either side of the well-traveled road running north of the capital, had the odor of animal refuse and decaying vegetation, which was no less odorous than the air in the town, reeking of tanned skins and rotting garbage once one was a short distance from the tree-covered castle grounds, the air outside the city seemed different.

It is the space, not the air. Nightshade's voice rang in his ear. *Out here, even with the presence of many two legged ones, there is room to run free. In the city, I am confined to a narrow stall, with no one to talk to.*

Pip had missed the silent conversations with Nightshade. Like Zohra, the black steed was accustomed to freedom. Pip sensed that he was becoming more like the two of them. He too felt confined in Lands End. Despite it being the only home he'd ever known, he felt that somehow he no longer belonged there.

I think I know how you feel, Pip thought back at him. *I, too, feel confined in the city, and find myself longing to be out here in the open land.*

Nightshade snorted. *Still too many two-legs here, though. We should travel to the lands in the far south.*

But, no one knows what lies in those lands.

That is the point. The black stallion snorted again. *Would you not like to know . . . to be the first to explore?*

In truth, he *would* like that very thing. But, he also had responsibilities. Responsibilities as Prince Valdar, heir to the throne of Pandara, and to his aunt and queen, Daphne, who had, as soon as she learned his identity, taken him to her bosom and become almost like a mother to him. He could not fail her, not as his queen, and not as his aunt. Then, there was his foster family. Uncle Auric, a simple leather worker, who had taught him the value of hard work, and Aunt Ludmilla, who had taught him to smile and be generous to others. Most importantly, though, there were his responsibilities to Zohra, his soul mate, and the unborn child she carried. Whenever he thought of that, his heart thudded so hard in his chest, he feared it would burst through. To imagine, Pip the foundling, the child picked upon by every other boy in Lands End, not only was he a royal prince—of Pandara and, through his father, Valcan, brother of Valdun, king of the fairy folk, he was a member of that royal family—but, he'd taken the most beautiful woman in the world as his wife, and that woman was now about to bear him a child.

As much as I would like to explore the world . . . and get out of the confines of the capital, I have responsibilities that make that . . . impossible at the moment.

Nightshade tossed his head. His way of expressing disdain for the customs and restrictions the two-legs put on themselves. But, mercifully, he didn't send his disdainful thoughts into Pip's mind. For that, Pip was grateful.

He turned his attention back to the countryside through which they rode. They'd gotten beyond the largest concentration of farms, with only the occasional hut set back far from the road marking human habitation. The land was undulating, with sporadic stands of conifers and a few small hills that jutted up like giant anthills scattered about. It was the nature of the terrain that had led Pip to approving his regimental commanders' requests to use it as a training area.

When the army had first been formed, they'd trained in the square near the castle guards' barracks. But, once both regiments were nearly fully manned—or, in the case of some of the fairy folk, like Vera and Tamara, womaned—the square would no longer accommodate them. Godfred and Melchor had taken the initiative to find a place with space enough, and had settled on this sparsely populated area, containing sufficient space for marching and exercise drills, a place for an archery range, and woods and hills to permit scouting and climbing practice. It had the added advantage of being sufficiently distant from inhabited farms so that they didn't have to fear animals or people wandering into the training area, in particular the areas where they drilled with ranged weapons like bows or catapults.

The sound of section leaders barking commands, and the shouted responses of soldiers, signaled their proximity to the training ground long before it came into sight.

Pip's chest swelled with pride as he viewed his army, *his* army, arrayed before him on the plain that bordered the road. The two regiments had set up their encampments opposite each other, with the road running between.

The soldiers' tents were arranged in five neat ranks, each rank containing twenty tents. The arrangement was identical on each side, each a mirror image of the other. Each tent housed two, meaning that excluding the ten soldiers on castle guard duty and twenty patrolling the western and southern regions, there were approximately 370 soldiers occupying the training ground.

The regimental commanders' tents were set up at the head of their subordinates' tents, with a large cook tent between each, and with tents for the officers flanking the cook tent. Each regiment had two battalions, and each battalion had four companies, so the officers' tents were set up five to either side, with the battalion commander closer to the cook tent. The regimental commanders' tents were simple affairs, large enough to accommodate staff meetings, but in no way ornate. Pip had been insistent that officers not be seen to have it any easier in the field than the lowest soldier. A large pole stood in front of each regimental commander's tent, atop which was the regimental flag, a simple blue rectangle containing a gold star with arrow-like rays extending in all directions and the number '1' or '2' depending upon the regiment. Vera had come up with the idea and, along with Tamara, had designed had supervised the sewing of the flags.

As Pip and Norbert entered the area, Godfred, commander of the First Regiment, emerged from his tent on the left side of the road. When he saw Pip, he rushed out into the middle of the road, his ample midsection jiggling as he ran. He stumbled to a halt directly in front of them, pulling himself erect and snapping a salute.

"Commander . . . your highness," he said. "Welcome. We not be expecting you."

Pip returned the salute. He swung his leg over and dismounted.

"Colonel Godfred," he said. "My apologies for not warning you of our visit, it was a last minute decision."

Godfred straightened his tunic and brushed imaginary dust from his shoulders.

"No matter, sir, we be glad you visit." He looked up at the sky. "There be a few hours before evening meal, would you like to inspect the training. I think Melchor be at the archery range."

"I would like that," Pip said. "Norbert, get someone to set out tents up and see to our equipment, and then join us at the archery range."

"Yessir," Norbert said, saluting sharply before turning toward the horses. He stopped suddenly and turned back. "Uh, Colonel Godfred, sir, which way is the stable."

"It be just beyond the camp, downwind of us." Godfred pointed. After Norbert had mounted, taking the reins of Nightshade and the pack horse and trotted off, Godfred turned back to Pip. "He be a fine soldier, that one, sir."

"That he is, but I have been thinking that he needs to get more field experience."

"Aye, and what be you havin' in mind for the lad?"

Pip laid a finger on his nose. "I have yet to really decide. I was hoping you and Colonel Melchor would be able to advise me on that."

"Aye, sir, and I be talkin' to Melchor and we get back to you."

"Thank you, Colonel Godfred. I knew I could depend on you." The rest of their journey to the area where a group of men were firing arrows at targets pinned to bales of hay took place in silence. The men, some of them quite good marksmen, some not so good, were working under the watchful eye of Bordin, a hunter from Pandara's north, and an expert with the bow. Colonel Melchor, a gaunt version of Godfred, and his best friend, stood by watching closely. When he saw Pip, he trotted to him, stopping six feet away and saluting so sharply his body seemed to vibrate.

"Sir, so glad you come to visit us," he said. "You be wantin' to see how good Bordin be teachin' the men, uh, and a few women, how to use the bow?"

Pip smiled briefly. While Norbert had, after working as his aide for a few months, totally erased all traces of the peasantry from his speech, Godfred and Melchor had come from peasant stock, were proud of it, and steadfastly refused to adopt the language used by the royals.

"I would like that very much," Pip responded. Then, he noticed the worry lines on Melchor's forehead. "Something else is bothering you, colonel?"

Melchor scratched at his thinning brown hair. A look of uncertainty creased his narrow face.

"Aye, sir," he said. "It be impossible to get anything past you, for sure. I do have a problem."

"Well," Pip said. "Tell me what it is."

"Uh, well, sir . . . it be one of the men, Sandrin be his name. He be something of a slacker, that one, and yesterday, he gave lip to his sergeant."

Pip's brows came together as he stared at the skinny colonel. He'd never known him to hesitate in the performance of his duties, and when he'd been a senior officer in the old castle guard, he'd had a reputation as something of a disciplinarian.

"I don't understand," Pip said. "If a soldier has misbehaved, why do you not just appropriately punish him?"

"Uh, he claim to be a personal friend of yours, sir."

Pip's eyes widened. He had never been close with the other boys of Lands End, certainly none had ever called him friend—and then, he remembered. Sandrin, son of a rich farmer who owned land on the outskirts of Lands End. Sandrin, leader of the gang of boys who constantly tormented and teased him before his true origins were known. A friend indeed!

"I know the name," Pip said. "He lived in

Lands End, but I would hardly call him a friend. If, however, he *was* a friend, it would make no difference. An army needs discipline, and the rules must apply to all, without favor or exception. What punishment would any other soldier receive for the same offense?"

"Ah well, since it be a first offense," Melchor said. "The offender would be assigned a week of privy cleaning duty."

Pip smiled at the thought of the bully Sandrin having to scoop waste from the four-foot-deep toilet trenches. The amount of waste that nearly four hundred people and their accompanying animals produced on a daily basis was . . . his mind reeled at the thought . . . and the smell. It would serve Sandrin right, and while Pip would never publicly revel in his old enemy's discomfort, inside, he smiled broadly.

"Then, so be it," he said. "Mayhap this will teach him a lesson. If not, we might have to consider expelling him from the ranks. Pandara's new army does not need soldiers who are unable to control themselves."

Melchor smiled and glanced at his friend, Godfred. The two men exchanged knowing looks.

"Aye, sir," Melchor said. "I be getting the sergeant major on it this very evening right after evening meal."

"Good, now if you two colonels would show me the training, I would appreciate it," Pip said.

Charles Ray

THREE

Pip and Norbert only spent two days with the

army, inspecting the training, the living area, and talking to the rank and file, which was something Pip felt important because it gave the soldiers a sense that their officers cared about them.

At mid-afternoon of the third day after their departure, they once again rode in the shadow of the castle's towers.

Pip dismounted and handed his reins to Norbert.

"See to the horses and equipment, Norbert," he said. "And, then take yourself off for the rest of the day. Mayhap, you could visit your family."

"Are you sure you will not need me for

anything, sir?"

"Yes," Pip said. "I must consult with Councilor Galen about something very important. Unless there is an emergency, I will go to my quarters from there."

The young soldier saluted and rode off in the direction of the royal stable. Pip adjusted his sword and strode beneath the large arched gateway, nodding at the two guards who saluted him as he passed.

He walked through the reception hall, on through the audience chamber, and through a side door into a hallway usually used only by the castle staff and one other—and, it was that one other, Galen, the queen's councilor, with whom Pip wished to speak.

As he walked the dustless passage; for every nook and cranny of the castle was swept and dusted daily under the watchful eye of his foster mother, now the Lady Ludmilla, whose title was personal assistant to the queen, but whose duties were only vaguely defined, usually only whenever she found some other aspect of managing the castle that needed her attention, he darted glances over his shoulder. Despite having resided there for more than two years, and being Daphne's heir—which meant he would one day be king, a thought that made him shiver—he often felt an interloper. Deep within his breast he was still Pip, the little red haired foundling, foster child of Auric the leather worker and Ludmilla the baker of the best bread in all of Lands End. His boots rang against the stone floor with a hollow sound, a sound that echoed off the stone walls, as if it was mocking him for the interloper he often considered himself to be.

It was with a sense of relief that he finally arrived at the end of the hallway. He stood before an unassuming wooden door. He paused for a moment before finally knocking softly.

"Enter," a cracked voice said from beyond the door.

Pip pulled on the brass handle. The door opened with a squeaking sound. He stepped into the room.

The hallway had been only dimly lit by oil lamps set high along the walls at regular intervals, but this room was brightly lit from a combination of two lanterns at opposite ends of a large desk, its top laden with scrolls and leather bound books, and a large window behind the desk which stretched almost from floor to ceiling, that looked out upon the back garden of the castle.

Behind the desk sat an old man. He was hunched of shoulder, with a face as furrowed as the gullies and valleys of the western region of Pandara, and thin gray hair that was plastered to his liver-spotted skull. He marked his place in the book he'd been reading with a gnarled forefinger, and looked up, regarding Pip with watery blue eyes, squinting as if having difficulty seeing clearly.

Galen, councilor to Queen Daphne, and sometime teacher of the town's children, had aged in the short while Pip had lived in the castle. Once tall, and to young Pip, an imposing figure, he now seemed bent and frail.

"Master Galen," Pip said. "I hope I am not interrupting anything important."

Galen waved at a wooden chair to his right.

"Not at all, my boy," he said in his cracked, hoarse voice. "I always have time for my star student. Sit and talk with me for a while. Would you like a cup of tea? I can have a servant bring a pot."

"No, Master Galen. If you would like tea, please go ahead. I am not thirsty."

Pip could feel the old man's gaze penetrating through him. Galen might be frail of body, Pip knew that his mind was still as sharp as a finely forged sword, and that little escaped his notice.

Galen leaned forward, steepling his hands in front of his face and peering over his fingertips at Pip.

"Well, young Pip, you look as if you are carrying the burden of the world on your shoulders. What is troubling you?"

As Pip pushed his sword aside to sit he could not help but look with amazement at his aging mentor. He was indeed as sharp as ever.

"Mayhap not as big as all that, Master Galen, but I do have a few things that are troubling me."

Galen rubbed his chin, making a soft rasping sound.

"Hm, can it be that my young student is

worried that he will soon be a father?" Galen grinned and his eyes twinkled as Pip's ruddy complexion turned a darker red.

Pip's mouth dropped open. Of all the problems that had been plaguing him, the guilt that he wanted to get away from the city at the very time Zohra was about to give birth was the greatest. He wasn't sure if he was ready to be a father, if he was qualified for such an important role.

Galen, though, had always been someone he could talk to, someone who could advise him.

"It is not that I . . . oh, Master Galen, I am not sure I know how to be a father."

Galen chuckled.

"Pip, my lad, no man knows anything about being a father until he becomes a father." He waggled a bony forefinger at Pip. "And, even after he becomes a father, he knows nothing."

Pip's mouth dropped open. His cheeks turned darker.

"B-but, how am I to raise a child if I know nothing?"

Galen leaned back in his chair and folded his arms across his chest.

"Do you remember how Auric raised you?"

How well he remembered. Auric had always been there for him, even during the darkest days when he'd come home crying because the other boys in the town had been tormenting him.

"He was always kind," Pip said. "When I felt bad, he would take me to his workshop and let me help him work. And, he would listen when I told him how I felt. It always made me feel better. Auric, even though I was a foundling, was always a kind father."

"Do you think he had any special training to be a father; that he always knew what he was doing?"

"It always seemed so to me."

"Pip, Auric had no training in fatherhood," Galen said. "Until you were brought to him, he had never had anything to do with children. He and Ludmilla learned as you grew. The only secret they had was . . . love. They only sought to help you grow into the man you have become. Each day was new to them, as strange and unfamiliar to them as it was to you. Do you not think that Auric sometimes feared that he would do the wrong thing?"

"Uh, I do not know. He always seemed to know what he was doing."

"No, my son, he did not. No man does. He only did what in his heart he thought was the right thing, and hoped that he was right. That is the secret to being a good father. Love your children, and always seek to do what is best for them."

"You make it seem so simple, Master Galen."

"No, it is not simple." Galen shook his head. "It is the most challenging thing for a man to face, for he must act without knowing what is right, only what he *thinks* is right. He never knows until the child is grown."

Now, it was Pip's turn to shake his head.

"It sounds difficult . . . having to act without knowing what will happen."

"It *is* difficult, Pip; the most difficult thing for a person to face. More difficult even than facing another man in battle, for at least then you have some idea how the other will react. When you must raise a child, you never know what the outcome will be until many years later."

"I suppose I must try and remember the way Uncle Auric was with me," Pip said. Then, a scary thought popped into his mind. "But, my child is likely to have . . . powers like mine. Surely the challenges I will face are unlike the problems Aunt Auric and Aunt Ludmilla had with me. How am I to deal with that?"

Galen's brow furrowed in concentration.

"You make a good point there," he said. "Your powers did not manifest themselves until you were almost a man, and only then because of your exposure to your father's people. Mayhap you should consult your uncle Valdun. He might be able to give you advice on raising a . . . special child."

Pip brightened at the thought of his uncle, the king of the fairy folk in the Land of Fire. He'd not spoken to him for some time, since before the final confrontation with Tenkuk. He'd been thinking of taking Zohra to visit the fairy land, but the press of organizing the army, and then Zohra's pregnancy had made it impossible.

With Vera's tutelage, he'd developed his power of transportation, but had been reluctant to attempt it with Zohra in her present condition. It was too late in the day to make the journey now, even with his ability to transport. But, it was something he would have to do. Besides, he thought, maybe Valdun could give him advice on how to deal with his feelings of unease about being cooped up in town.

"That is a good idea, Master Galen," he said. "I must see to the Lady Zohra now, but on the morrow I will visit Valdun."

FOUR

Pip spent a quiet evening with Zohra. Over a light supper, he told her of his inspection of the regimental training, and afterwards they sat together in the garden near their chambers, enjoying the fragrance of the flowers and the chirping of the night insects.

Zohra was still sleeping when Pip woke up the next morning. He kissed her forehead lightly and eased out of bed so as not to awaken her. After a light breakfast, he checked and saw that she was still sleeping peacefully. Dressed in his dark green tunic and trousers, with the soft leather boots favored by the fairy folk, he slipped out to the back courtyard which was deserted in the early morning. His plan was to transport to the Land of Fire for a morning chat with his uncle, and return to Lands End in time for the midday meal.

Looking around to make sure he was unobserved, he let his arms hang limply at his side and, as Vera had instructed him, pictured in his mind the glade in which Valdun held court for the fairy folk—the People.

No matter how many times he did it, Pip never failed to be amazed at the process of transportation. Vera had tried to explain it to him, something about tuning into the life waves and flow around him and using his power to visualize where he wanted to be and then riding those waves. Her explanation might as well as have been in the language of the fishes for all Pip's understanding. All he knew was that he could *wish* himself to be somewhere, and there he would be. It was not, however, an instantaneous journey, and that was the part that Pip was both fascinated and horrified by.

For, in an instant, the scene around him would blink out of existence, to be replaced with a formless gray void that seemed to whip past him. He could not feel it, nor could he hear anything other than an almost inaudible humming in his ear. Vera had explained to him that the sense of the gray moving was actually him moving through the . . . transubstantial ether, she had called it; the substance that held all together and served as the link between one part of the universe and another. Wryly, Pip often wondered what would happen should two beings happen to occupy the same portion of transubstantial ether at the same time. Vera hadn't found his wondering amusing, and had assured him such a circumstance was unlikely in the extreme. Impossible would have been better odds in Pip's mind, but his cousin was adamant that it was safe, and in truth, he'd not had a mishap any of the times he'd done it. In fact, his ability to transport himself short distances had saved him during his fight with the tyrant Tenkuk.

Before he could wonder further about his means of travel, the gray void disappeared to be replaced by the luxurious verdant glade in Valdun's kingdom. Pip found himself standing in the same position he'd been in in the garden of the castle, but instead of the flowers and flagstones, he faced a giant throne made of rock, wood and entwined with pink, yellow, and white bell shaped flowers. Valdun, his flame-red hair now streaked with white, but still with a vigorous glow in his reddish skin, sprawled on the throne, regarding Pip with an expression that said he'd been expecting him.

"Welcome, Valdar, son of Valcan and Daria," he said in his deep voice. "Why has thee sought my counsel this morn?"

He *had* expected me, Pip thought without much surprise, for his uncle was the most powerful of fairies. *I wonder if I have the ability to read thoughts.* Pip wanted to ask his uncle if this was so.

Instead, he inclined his head slightly and stepped forward until he was close enough to peer into his red eyes.

"Uncle, I come because I have had troubling thoughts, and I have no one I can share them with who might understand, except mayhap you."

Valdun tugged at the collar of his tunic as he gazed down at Pip. His brow furrowed. Slowly, he stood, and sighed deeply.

"I think I know what thee thinks, what bothers thee," he said. "But, even though I am a father, I must confess that I do not know how to advise thee."

Pip blinked. On the one hand, it did not surprise him that Valdun knew what was on his mind. Although he didn't think that he could actually *read* his thoughts, he knew the fairy king just *knew* things. He had not, though, expected him to be unable to give him the answers he sought. If Valdun, the most powerful being Pip knew, didn't have the answers to his problem, then he was indeed in deep trouble. Valdun waved toward two logs that sat at the base of the hill upon which his throne sat. Pip followed, and seated himself on the smaller log, set about an inch lower than Valdun's in a gesture of respect.

"If you are unable to help me, what am I to do? There is no one else with your wisdom."

Valdun sat and brushed nonexistent wrinkles from his trousers.

"That is not true. There is one among us who

is far wiser than I. Mayhap he can help thee."

Pip looked at him with confusion.

"Doest thee not remember thy mentor, Hermes?" Valdun said. Annoyance momentarily flashed across his face.

"Yes, I remember him," Pip said. "He is a water spirit. How can he help me with raising my child?"

Valdun's frown deepened. He sighed.

"Thee knows little about Hermes. He is more than a mere water spirit. He is the wisest sage in the Land."

"Then, I must speak to him." Pip sat back on the log, his back against the soft earth.

Valdun closed his eyes. *Hermes, didst thee hear?*

Hermes, his white hair framing his pale face, suddenly appeared in front of Pip.

"I heard thee, Valdun," Pip's former mentor said in his liquid voice. "Hello, Valdar, it has been a long time since our little . . . adventure. How hast thee fared since?"

Pip cleared his throat. He'd always felt a bit intimidated when in the presence of Hermes, more so even than he'd been when practicing weapons or fighting with Walu the ogre, Gork and Gelum, the gnomes, or Nork, the troll. While they had worked him hard, leaving many bruises in the process, Hermes had simply towered over him mentally, never raising his voice, always stoic and quiet, nevertheless, of all the People, he was the one who could cause Pip to quiver inside.

"Uh, I . . . as you mayhap know, I am now married . . . and, will soon be a father-"

"And thy heart is filled with fear at that prospect."

Not a question, simply a statement of fact that got right to the heart of the matter. Now, Hermes, Pip was convinced, *could* read his thoughts.

"Aye," he said. "I fear that more even than facing an enemy in battle. I know naught of raising a child."

Hermes walked over and sat next to Pip. He placed a slender hand on his shoulder.

"Lad, no one can teach thee how to be a father," he said gently. "Thee must simply love thy . . . child, answer the many questions . . . it will have." Hermes sneaked a peek at Valdun, who looked on sternly.

"But, what if my child has powers like mine? How will . . . what do I do about that?" Pip protested.

"It is not a matter of what if," Hermes said. "Thy good wife is an Avian, and while the people of her kind do not have fully the same powers as we Folk, they do possess the power to communicate with the birds."

"Uh, I did not know this," Pip said.

Hermes patted Pip's shoulder, and then squeezed the developed musculature.

"My thee hast grown much since we last met."

Get on with thy story. Valdun's voice growled in Hermes' brain.

"Ah, yes," Hermes said. "The Avians do not think of this ability as special. They believe all creatures have such ability, so they do not talk about it."

"Okay, so my wife has special power, but what does that mean for our child?"

"Consider, Pip, thy mother was Pandaran, a mundane, but they father was of the Folk. Thee has more power than any other of the Folk, including King Valdun. Your . . . child will combine your power and that of Zohra of the Avians. H-, it will surely be powerful, mayhap even more powerful than thee."

"B-but, how am I to-"

"As any father of any species would," Valdun cut in. His voice was firm, but gentle. "Thee must protect thy child, teach what thee knowest, and trust in thy good judgment. That is all that a father can do. Fortunately for us males, the mothers have the final say in nurturing of the young."

Pip looked helplessly from one to the other. His mind spun like dandelion spores in a breeze. These were the two most powerful people he knew. How could they not have answers for him?

"I do not understand," he said. "You both have such power. You can control the elements, move from one place to another without effort; how can you not know the secrets of fatherhood?"

Both men chuckled.

"That, my young friend, is the one secret of

the universe that no one has the answer to," Hermes said. "Why are male and female so different in many ways, yet the same in others? I do not know, Valdun doest not know, and thee shall never know."

Pip could only shrug. If two such wise ones took this view, there was little else he could do. Valdun validated this view immediately.

"We males have little to do once we have contributed our seed, but go along for the journey. The mother is the pilot in that journey. Mayhap the best we can do is observe carefully, and remain silent until our counsel is sought, and then attempt to give the best answer we can. Most importantly, we must endeavor never to do harm."

Both men looked at each other, smiled and inclined their heads as if sharing some profound secret. Pip saw the exchanged glances, but decided he'd heard all he was to hear from them on this matter. Then, another thought blossomed in his mind.

"You said that Zohra's people, the Avians, have the power to communicate with birds; does this mean they are somehow related to the Folk?"

Again, Hermes and Valdun shared a look.

Mayhap it is time to tell him.

Hermes nodded at Valdun's suggestion—nay, as Valdun was king, his royal command.

"Pip," he said. "Thee will recall during our training sessions, I said that at a time in the long past, Folk and the people of Pandara were related and lived together?"

"Yes, you said that Pandarans stopped believing in the powers, and our two people began living apart, but what does this have to do with Zohra's people?"

Hermes arranged the hem of the silver robe he always wore and settled back. Pip recognized this as the beginning of a lone tale. Hermes was as avid a storyteller as Councilor Galen, and Pip, when he studied under him, had found his stories fascinating. He looked anxiously at Hermes, silently willing him to commence, and was not disappointed.

"I did not tell thee the whole story," Hermes said. "For it was not just the Folk and the people of Pandara who were part of the whole. There were others; the Barbarians, the people of Draconia and Avia, and people from lands far to the south whose names have been forgotten with the passage of time. All beings lived together in harmony. This was before the time of my father's father's father, before the people of Pandara and Barbaria foreswore magic and the powers of the Folk became stronger.

A shadow of sadness passed across Hermes' face.

"It was a time of darkness, and war broke out between and among many of the different groups. Ye of Pandara took the road of peace, while the Barbarians became warlike. Each went a separate way, and for a long time there was no contact among them. We had just begun to reach out to the Pandarans when thy mother, the beautiful lady Daria, was saved from the wolves by Valcan, brother of our king. It had long before that encounter been foretold that there would come a day when a child would appear, and that child would again unite the people of the world in peace. I . . . we . . . think, Valdar, that *ye* are that child. Ye have already fulfilled parts of the prophecy; the defeat of the tyrant Tenkuk and peace between Pandara and Barbaria, making peace with Draconia without going to war, and uniting with the Avians through marriage to Zohra."

When Hermes paused to take a breath, Pip leaned forward.

"But, what of the unknown people beyond Barbaria," he said. "How am I to make peace with them? I know not where they live."

"The prophecy is ancient, young one, and not always clear in meaning. Ye will know what to do when the time comes. Now, ye must return to your wife. I sense that she wonders about thy location."

Pip sighed heavily. As much as he enjoyed the reunion with his old teacher, none of his questions had really been answered. Instead, he was left with even more questions. He stood and dusted the seat of his pants.

"Yes, I suppose you are right. I must not keep the Lady Zohra waiting. I did promise her I would share the midday meal with her."

With that, he closed his eyes and let his arms hang loosely at his sides.

There was a low, rushing sound, like air

leaking from a bladder, and he was no longer there, leaving Valdun and Hermes sitting looking at each other, Hermes with a look of feigned innocence as Valdun glared.

Charles Ray

FIVE

Pip found himself standing in the same spot from which he'd departed, and the sun had only inched upwards two hand spans since. He had no need of the sun, though, because the growling sound from his stomach told him it was near time for the midday meal.

He hurried off in search of Zohra.

She wasn't in their bedchamber. A passing servant, though, informed Pip that the Lady Zohra was in the garden off the main hall with Queen Daphne.

He found the two women sitting at a table set for three in the center of the garden. They were in lively conversation that stopped as soon as he appeared. He stopped and bowed slightly at the waist.

"Your Majesty, Lady Zohra," Pip said. "Forgive my late arrival. I had urgent business to attend."

His words, so correct and formal, must have sounded as inane to the two women as they had to him even as they were spewing forth. They both laughed, Zohra holding a hand over her swollen midsection.

Daphne waved her delicate hand toward the empty chair at the table.

"Sit, dear Pip," she said, still fighting to stifle laughter. "You are not late. How could you be, since you were not informed of our plans in advance?"

"I-I just thought--"

"He is so cute when he is nervous," Zohra said, cutting him off. "And he becomes so formal in his speech. It is really quite amusing."

Daphne patted Zohra's hand. Pip sat across from them, his brow wrinkled, and a look of total confusion on his face.

"Yes, and then he gets a look like a wood bear," Daphne said. "His eyes get round, and his brow wrinkles up. You are right, Zohra dear, he is quite cute."

Peevishness began to replace confusion as Pip realized that his wife and his aunt were having fun at his expense. His expression darkened.

"I was only being polite, as is expected of the heir to Pandara's throne, Your Majesty," he said. "And, as is expected from a husband toward his wife, Lady Zohra."

Their laughter stopped suddenly. Two pairs of eyes regarded Pip seriously for all of two heartbeats. Then, Daphne clapped her hands over her mouth and began laughing again. Zohra didn't even try to cover her laughter, as she leaned back in her chair, her hands clasped over her jiggling stomach. Pip tried to maintain his stony glare, but in the face of their obvious mirth, found it impossible. Besides, he thought, they were absolutely right. He'd sounded like a pompous jackass.

"Very well," he said, holding his hands up in surrender. "You two are, as usual, right. I apologize . . . for being a jackass. Now, how is that?"

Daphne smiled up at him. "That is much, much better," she said. "Now, come here and give your aunt a kiss, hug this beautiful wife of yours, and sit down and join us for the midday meal."

Pip did as instructed, lingering when he pulled Zohra into his arms so that he could nuzzle her silken hair, and finally taking his seat facing the two of them—two of the three most important women in his life. No, he reminded himself, mustn't forget his cousin, Vera. After his foster mother Ludmilla, Vera had been the first person of the opposite gender to pay him any attention, and for that she would always occupy a special place in his thoughts.

"So, husband," Zohra said. "Where did you

rush off to this morning?"

Pip's first reaction was to change the subject. Not that he would consider lying to Zohra, or to anyone for that matter, but because he didn't want her to know that he was feeling misgivings about becoming a father. He hesitated, though, for only a heartbeat.

"I paid a quick visit to King Valdun," he said.

"I do hope you gave him greetings from me," Daphne said.

Pip gulped as he remembered that he'd forgotten to even mention his aunt to Valdun, knowing how much the king respected his fellow sovereign. Recovering his composure, he confessed that the issue he'd wished to discuss with his fairy uncle was such that he'd forgotten. Then, he told them both his reason for the visit, fearing that Zohra would be upset at the news. He was surprised when, instead of being angry or upset, she favored him with a sympathetic look, and reached across the table and patted his hand gently.

"So, my fearless husband is fearful at the prospect of being a father?" There was a mischievous twinkle in her eyes as she shared a conspiratorial look with Daphne. "Did I not tell you, Queen Daphne that it would be thus?"

Pip's aunt laughed and wiped at her lips with a fine linen napkin.

"Yes you did, child," she said. "And, I must confess that your wisdom is greater than my own. I do not understand why this would be a cause for fear. Pip, you should be rejoicing that you will soon have a son or daughter."

"I . . .," Pip struggled to find the proper thing to say; confused by the fact that both women seemed to find his discomfort amusing. "I am not sure that I know how to be a proper father, so I sought Valdun's wise counsel."

"Pip, my dear one," Zohra said. "No man can tell you how to be a father, not even one who *is* father to many children. It is something you will have to learn every day." She turned to Daphne, still with the impish smile on her face. "This is why we Avians only entrust the true rearing of children to the women. Men only become useful once a child is weaned and prepared to learn the things that men *do* know how to do."

"I have no experience with children," Daphne said. "But, my observations of the people of my kingdom would seem to bear you out. When the children are very young, the men seem to be more of a burden to the mothers than the children themselves."

"Yes, for the first six years, the men are useless. They are like an extra child at times."

Pip looked from one woman to the other. From the smiles on their faces, he sensed that they might be joking, but recalling his own early years, his foster father, Auric, didn't seem to be around much, only taking an active part in his life after he was old enough to attend the classes taught by Galen.

"So," he said. "I have no role in rearing my own child until he or she is no longer really a child? That does not seem right."

"Fear not, husband," Zohra said. "There will be much for you to do, but you will learn what you need to do when you need to do it."

"And, how am I to learn this?"

Zohra patted his hand again.

"I will teach you, of course."

"B-but, you are a woman, what do you know about being a father?"

"Ah, sweet Pip," Daphne said, laughing so she could scarcely form the words. "You do have a lot to learn. I have never been a mother, but even I know that women have been instructing men on everything since time began."

As Pip pondered the meaning—and, perhaps the wisdom—of her words, a servant came out and bowed low to Daphne.

"Your majesty," the man said. "There be someone requesting an urgent audience."

"Please tell that *someone* that I will grant them an audience as soon as I have finished the midday meal with my nephew and his wife."

"B-but, your majesty, h-he said it was most urgent. H-he is a representative of the Kingdom of Alluria, he said."

"Kingdom of Alluria? I have never heard of such a kingdom." Daphne's brow furrowed and she half closed her eyes. "Very well, then, Malcolm, show our visitor here, and have someone bring another place setting."

"Y-you will be eating w-with him?" The servant looked mortified. "He is a strange l-looking p-person, Your M-majesty."

"I suspect we will also look strange to him, Malcolm. Nevertheless, escort him here." She looked at Pip and her lips turned upward. Her eyes twinkled again as they had done when Pip first arrived to join her and Zohra. "My nephew is quite capable of protecting me. Are you not, nephew?"

"Why, of course . . . Your Majesty," Pip said.

But, a tingle of feeling at the back of his neck caused him to wonder.

Charles Ray

SIX

The visitor from Alluria was indeed strange.

At least a foot taller than Councilor Galen, who trailed close behind him, he was as thin as the reeds that grew in the shallows of the lakes of Pandara. His hair was thin and wispy, sticking out from his head at all angles like white feathers. He had a thin face with a greenish-tinted complexion, with sunken cheeks and a long, curved nose that resembled a crow's beak, which, when combined with his unkempt hair, gave him the appearance of a large, starving eagle. Despite his emaciated, deprived appearance, though, he was dressed in a silken robe that whispered against the stones of the floor as he walked, no glided, Pip thought, across them. Around his waist, wrists and neck was a fortune in gold, silver, and precious gems that sparkled when the sunlight struck them.

As the stranger came nearer, Pip noticed that the resemblance to an eagle was further enhanced by the unblinking yellow eyes that peered down at him as if he was prey waiting to be devoured.

The stranger stopped and bowed low, folding in half at the waist, and dipping his head below his knees.

After a long time, with the man still bowed and unmoving, discomfort showed on Daphne's face. Although a hereditary monarch accustomed to her subjects bowing to her, she'd never seen anyone bow so low, or hold the position so long. Finally, when she could take it no longer, she cleared her throat.

"Please, kind sir," she said. "You may stop bowing."

The man stood upright, looking at her dispassionately with his unblinking yellow eyes. He reminded Pip of the desert viper, which also had unblinking yellow eyes. The man made him uncomfortable.

"What is your business with the queen?" he asked.

The man's gaze shifted from Daphne to Pip, but his expression did not otherwise change. His thin lips remained closed. Pip felt the heat rise to his cheeks. The impertinent fool was ignoring him. Just as he opened his mouth to speak, Daphne raised a hand in a subtle gesture to stop him.

"Yes, kind sir," she said in a soft voice. "What is the nature of your visit to my castle?"

"I am Moldor, Herald to Her Royal Highness Princess Miko, Sovereign of Demesne of Alluria," he said as if reciting a lesson in school. "I come to this demesne at command of my princess to seek help in important matter."

Spots of color appeared in Daphne's cheeks, and anger flared in her sky blue eyes.

"This, sir is not a *demesne*," she said icily. "It is the *Kingdom* of Pandara."

"Aunt, er, Your Majesty," Pip said. "What is a demain?"

She smiled at Pip's mangled pronunciation of the ancient word. "D*emesne*, D. E. M. E. S. N. E., is an ancient term for land held by a ruler but worked by a commoner. In many realms, the one who holds the throne also owns everything." She turned back to Moldor, her smile disappearing. "Here in Pandara, the people are the owners of their own land. The sovereign holds only the responsibility for the protection of every subject."

The green complexion of the man's gaunt cheeks darkened. His white eyebrows quivered, and he looked momentarily confused. Then his oval eyes widened.

"Ah, I see. Please forgive mistake. In my land is different. Princess Miko own everything and everyone."

"Everyone; you mean even the people are owned by this . . . princess?" Pip's eyes were round.

"Is what I said," Moldor said evenly. "People part of demesne. Ruler own demesne."

"Buh, buh--"

Daphne again waved her hand, bringing an end to Pip's sputtering.

"Our neighbors in Barbaria had a similar custom," she said. "There, under the rule of the cruel King Ostro and his predecessors, the nobles owned the land, which was worked by the peasants, who were little more than slaves. When Tenkuk slew Ostro things remained the same as far as land ownership was concerned, but life for the common people became even harsher. How, under the Council of Nobles, things are becoming better for the people of Barbaria . . . or so I am led to believe."

"It is true, Your Majesty," Pip said. "The nobles have come to realize that a man who owns his property will work harder than one who is but a tenant. They now sell land to the peasants and then tax them on their production. It is still somewhat harsh; the nobles profit from the land without taking any risk; but, they at least offer the peasants protection with Barbaria's army."

"Which is comprised of the sons of the peasants who are required by the council to serve," Zohra said. Her voice dripped with sarcasm.

"Aye, it is true. Barbaria's army is not voluntary as is ours, but I have visited once or twice, and the men are well fed and well led, and most seem to like the life of a soldier, which is much better than the back-breaking toil of working a farm."

Zohra made a sniffing noise. Moldor's head swiveled from side to side, following the conversation.

"What is tax?" he asked when they stopped talking and looked back to him.

"Tax is, never mind, Moldor," Daphne said. "What is this important matter your princess seeks help with, and why do you come to Pandara seeking it?"

"In Alluria, we are having problem," he said. "Is problem that not even mighty army of demesne can handle. We are having heard of mighty warrior you have in . . . Pandara. Princess Miko is sending me to ask for your warrior's service."

Pip felt his heart flutter and his pulse begin to race. Even though the man was extremely strange, and made him a trifle nervous, he was asking for Pip's service—he had to be the warrior the man was referring to. He fought to keep his emotions from showing on his face.

Daphne, on the other hand, appeared completely unaffected by the man or his words.

"And, just what service is this warrior to perform for your princess?"

If Moldor noticed the iciness in Daphne's words, he didn't let it show. His face remained impassive.

"Is needing warrior to vanquish demon," he said.

"Demon? Did I hear you correctly; you said demon?" Daphne's eyes blazed—with fear or anger, which it was Pip could not tell, but her voice was tight.

Moldor bowed his head. "Yes, I am saying demon. Is causing much problem for demesne. Farmers are losing goats and other animals. Is not able to producing enough food for peoples. Soon we are having starvation."

"Does your king-, demesne not have an army?" she asked.

"Army of Alluria is not having to fight for long time. Is mainly used to keep peasants under control. We are sending one unit to fight monster, but they run back to capital in big panic. Say big demon attack them, make them afraid."

"Except for our recent encounter with our neighbor, Barbaria, we here in Pandara have been a peaceful people. We have little experience in making war. I would think you would be better served by the army of Barbaria—they have much more experience at war than do we."

Moldor smiled. His lips remained tightly

compressed; merely turning up at the corners.

"And yet, you are defeating them," he said. "Yes, we are hearing of this even in Alluria. We are also hearing that your army has leader with great power, and some of your soldiers come from the place of burning mountains."

That disclosure caused a return of Pip's initial nervousness about the man. He'd obviously had access to good intelligence about Pandara in general, and Pip specifically. His intuition told him that this was not for reasons of benevolence.

He looked at Queen Daphne, his eyebrows arched in a request to speak. She nodded.

"What is the nature of this demon?" he asked.

"Is not knowing. No one has seen the demon."

"Then, how do you know it is even a demon?"

Moldor looked at Pip as he would the bottom of his shoe after walking through a pig sty.

"What else can eat a whole cow or goat, or belch fire from a cave," he said. "You are knowing something that can do this other than demon?"

Pip knew many things that could eat a whole cow; the large black bears of the northern mountains, the dragons of Draconia, but to his knowledge, only certain of the Folk could manipulate fire—and even they could not *breathe* fire.

"Okay," Pip said. "But, what do you expect me, I mean, our warrior, to be able to do."

Moldor's left eyebrow twitched, and he stared deeply at Pip.

"We are hearing that your warrior has special power. Since regular army is not able to defeat demon, is hoping that warrior's special power can."

Pip and Daphne shared a look.

"Pip, you are not thinking--"

"You cannot do this," Zohra broke in.

"But, I *can* do it, Zohra, Aunt Daphne," he said. "In fact, I am probably the only one who can."

Moldor gazed quizzically at Pip, a half smile on his face.

"Excuse please, but why does small boy want to go on dangerous mission?"

Daphne and Zohra laughed. Pip's reddish complexion turned scarlet. Before he could respond to the stranger's comments, Daphne recovered her composure and leaned forward.

"Herald Moldor," she said. "Allow me to present Crown Prince Valdar, who also happens to be the commander of the army of Pandara, and is the warrior with the special power of whom you speak."

Moldor's stony expression cracked for a heartbeat as he stared at Pip. Then, the stony mask was back.

"Apologies, Your Highness," he said. "You

look so young; too young to do things I have heard you can do."

Pip had long decided that the best way to handle people when they learned of his powers was to be fully open.

"I am only half Pandaran," he said. "My father was of the Folk of the Land of Fire. It is from him that I inherited my power. If you are familiar with the Folk, you will know that they are long lived, and youthful in appearance even into advanced age."

That last was only partially true, but it tended to placate those who worried about Pip's youth—thankfully, he encountered few such in Pandara, but the Barbarians, some of them, still clung to old traditions and beliefs, and now it seemed, so did the Allurians. A new people, in the unexplored lands south of Barbaria, and who knew what lay beyond them! His blood sang at the thought of exploring.

"Yes," Moldor was saying, when Pip's attention was brought back to him. "I have heard of Fairies. Would explain why you look so young. Now, is only to ask if you will help?"

Pip was vibrating in his chair, certain that both Zohra and Daphne could feel the excitement radiating off his body in waves. *Of course* he would help. Not that he was quite sure what the Allurian wanted him to do, but it meant adventure, and for now, that was quite enough.

Zohra's hand tightening on his wrist brought him out of his reverie. When he looked at her he could see worry in her dark eyes.

"Of course, we always seek to help our neighbors," Daphne said. "And, even though Barbaria separates us, I consider the people of Alluria neighbors. Before I agree to send help, though, I must know more of your problem."

Moldor seemed at ease dealing with Daphne's cool, confident demeanor. He turned to face her and described Alluria's problem.

Alluria, a small kingdom, just beyond the mountains that formed the southern border of Barbaria, long and narrow, being mostly a mountain range that ran from the west down to the Great Sea, was populated by people who mostly kept to themselves. They had a narrow strip of coast, and from the tiny villages clinging to the rocky shore, their boats ventured out into the sea to fish. They raised sheep and goat, subsisting on their milk and meat, and trading their luxurious fur with the southern Barbarians. They had been at peace for many generations, only having to deal with the occasional bandit raid from Barbaria—which was why they hadn't asked their Barbarian neighbors for help— until farmers started reporting missing animals. When they found the remains of a few unfortunate beasts, scraps of bloody fur and bone, they knew they were dealing with something more dangerous than bandit raids. The small Allurian army was dispatched to take care of the situation. The soldiers followed a bloody trail of death and destruction; fortunately, the demon hadn't developed a taste for other than four-legged creatures; until they came to a series of caverns deep in the western mountains. At the mouth of the largest, the soldiers in the vanguard were suddenly overcome by a sense of dread, which seemed to ripple through the ranks. Not wishing to displease their sovereign, and reluctant to admit fear, they pressed on, but as they did so, the sense of dread only heightened. The cave in which they found themselves was high-ceilinged, with dim light from a kind of fungus clinging to the rocky walls. To add to the sense of doom, the place reeked of a sulfuric smell. The soldiers hadn't gone more than a few hundred yards into the cave, when they were greeted by a loud roar—a sound like a thunderstorm—and gouts of flame erupting from the walls to their front. This overcame any fear they might have had of their sovereign. The army turned and fled, screaming, all the way back to the capital. A sense of fear and desperation had settled over the land, and, with nowhere else to turn, Moldor had been dispatched to seek the assistance of the fabled warrior of Pandara who had defeated the evil Tenkuk, and who was reported to possess special powers like no other man.

When Moldor had finished his story, Daphne sat back, a contemplative look on her face. Pip watched her closely. He was always amazed at her ability to retain her composure, even under the most trying circumstances, and wanted to learn to do the same. Most importantly, in this instance, he wanted to know if she would grant the stranger's request, and send him to aid these newly discovered people and their unknown land.

Pip didn't think he could stand the suspense another moment. He was on the verge of saying something, when Daphne finally spoke.

"Your situation does indeed sound dire," she said. "While I am not at all sure what we can do to make things better, it is not our custom to ignore the plight of others." She turned to Pip and Zohra. "I know that I am placing an imposition upon you, my children, but I must ask Pip to prepare immediately to travel to Alluria and see what we can do to help in their hour of need."

SEVEN

Pip had expected Zohra to be disappointed at his leaving for the journey to Alluria. He had not been prepared for her to be furious.

She sat in the middle of their large canopied bed, her arms folded across her midsection, and her elbows resting on her knees. Her eyes blazed with anger and her face, normally a light tan from her exposure to the sun was as red as Pip's was normally, but on her was a signal that she was angry. As if he couldn't tell her mood from her expression, when he crossed the threshold, she picked up a pillow and flung it at him.

"How dare you," she said in a voice that quivered with emotion. "I am near to presenting you with a child, and you volunteer to go running off on some foolish errand. How could you?"

As she said that last, she flung herself back against the remaining pillow, put her arms over her face and cried.

Pip rushed to the bed and knelt, placing his hands on her heaving shoulders. She buried her face against his shoulder, still shaking.

"Zohra, my heart, my only one," he said softly. "It is not that I want to . . . that I do not want to stay by your side. But . . . I have a responsibility, and . . . the queen has decided."

She pulled back and beat her fist against his chest.

"Yes, but do not tell me it is not your wish. For the past few weeks, I have noticed that you have been restless, and today, when you expressed your fear at becoming a father, I . . ."

He rubbed her back, tracing lazy circles, pulling her against his chest until her shaking eased.

"It is true that I miss the action of the field, and am restless here in the city. You must remember, though, I spent my first years here, and it was most unpleasant . . . except for the presence of Uncle Auric and Aunt Ludmilla, and of course, Galen . . . so, when I discovered the world outside, it was--"

Zohra put a finger to his lips.

"I know, Pip, I know. When I first came here to Lands End, I longed for nothing more than to return to my home in Avia. Now that I have become accustomed to it, though, I can think of no other place I would rather call home. But, I too miss the action and adventure of being in the field."

"There is more," Pip said. "It is true that I fear being a father. I look forward to it, but at the same time, I am afraid that I am not ready and will do everything wrong."

It was her turn now to comfort him. She put her arms around him and rubbed his back.

"I know, my dearest, I know. I fear becoming a mother at times."

"B-but, I thought you said--"

"Oh, I know what I said, and I meant it then. But, there are still times when I am not sure I . . . oh, Pip, do you not know? No one knows *how* to be a parent until they become one. Babies do not come with a set of instructions. But, I am certain, that we can be good parents as long as we work together, love each other, and love our child."

"Oh, Zohra, that is one thing you need have no fear of. I have never loved anyone before you, and can love no one like I love you. I am sure I . . . I *know* I will love our child."

She leaned back, her hands gripping his shoulders, looking up into his eyes. He felt his heart flutter at what he saw; he saw in her eyes the love she bore.

"Then, my husband," she said. "You must do what you must do."

He took her hand, holding her fingertips to his lips, brushing them lightly.

"I will be back before the child is born. I promise you that."

EIGHT

At sunrise of the next day, before most of the people of Lands End were bustling about, Pip assembled his traveling party in the forecourt of the castle.

He'd debated the merits of taking a large portion of the army, but not knowing the situation in Alluria—Moldor said everyone believed there was only *one* demon—and, the need to keep a defensive capability in Pandara, argued for a smaller party.

His first inclination had been to leave Vera in charge of the army, but she dug in her heels, insisting that despite the new feelings of friendship between Pandarans and the Folk, the soldiers would be reluctant to accept a fairy as commander, and a female at that. Her main argument, though, was that there was no way she was allowing her cousin to go traipsing off to some unknown land to fight an unknown demon without her. He, therefore, placed Godfred, the elder of his two regimental commanders, in temporary command of the army. Once Tamara learned that Vera was going, she insisted that she too should be included. Norbert begged to be included. Pip first declined, until the young man reminded him that he'd accompanied him during the mission to rescue Queen Daphne when she'd been kidnapped by Tenkuk, and he'd acquitted himself well. With Moldor's entourage, four burly, green-skinned spearmen who spoke only in unintelligible grunts and stayed to themselves, that brought them to nine. When pack animals were included, it was still a larger group than Pip thought necessary, but there was nothing to be done about it.

They made good time the first day, making it halfway across the Great Desert by mid-afternoon. They found a flat area near a large rock outcropping that offered some relief from the incessant heat of the sun. Knowing they'd only make the border area between Barbaria and the desert by dark, and unsure of the security situation, Pip suggested they stop and make camp.

Moldor grumbled, complaining that they should continue their journey, but a glare from Vera quieted him, much to the amusement of the four soldiers accompanying him, Pip noticed.

The next morning, after striking camp and resuming their journey, Moldor rode near Pip, glancing furtively at Vera who rode a few yards in front.

"Is always so angry this one?" he asked.

"She is not angry," Pip said. "She just does not like to waste time with argument when the person arguing is not logical."

Moldor's face screwed up in concentration.

"Ah, I am seeing. Wanting to go on without knowing where we could make camp was not logical."

"As long as you keep things like that in mind, you should have no problem getting along with Vera."

Moldor rubbed at his chin.

"Am hoping to do just that," he said.

The green two-legged one has no chance with Vera. Nightshade's deep voice was loud in Pip's mind.

I know this, Pip responded in kind. *But, it is not my concern. Vera is more than capable of putting the Allurian in his place.*

It is not your cousin who worries me.

What do you have to worry about?

Nightshade didn't answer. He snorted and twisted his head around, his dark eye glaring at Pip.

Pip shrugged and turned his attention back to the surrounding desert. As they neared the border of Barbaria, the desert became less bleak, with dark plants taking the place of the skeletal cacti that stood lonely sentinel in the sandy waste.

The first indication that they were in Barbaria was a haphazardly constructed wooden rail fence and a well-worn trail. Beyond the fence a herd of the wooly, long-horned cattle favored by the Barbarians for meat and hide, grazed contentedly, under the watchful eye of a lanky boy who stood atop a large boulder with a long wooden staff in his hand. The boy wore an over-jacket and trousers made from the tanned hide of the cattle he guarded. Unlike his visits to Barbaria during Tenkuk's reign of terror, when the people of the countryside were wary of all strangers, and would either hide from them or attack them, the boy smiled and waved at them as they rode past.

Settlements increased the deeper into the country they rode, with those living closer to Gondwana, the capital city, more prosperous than the outlying ones. While their group elicited stares and comments as they rode through the small villages, there was no sense of unease. This pleased Pip. It meant that the relationship with their once antagonistic neighbor had indeed changed, and for the better.

"I think we should bypass the capital," Pip called up to Vera. She nodded her agreement.

"Why do we not visit city?" Moldor asked.

"It is having nice inn. Is good place to get meal and spend night."

From his grumbling when they'd made camp in the desert, Pip had gotten the sense that Moldor wasn't one aching for the adventure of the wild. The man was fastidious beyond belief, constantly brushing at every dust mote, swatting at the insects that swarmed near the fire, and complaining that the ground beneath his blanket was too hard. The Allurian soldiers, or Pip had at least chosen to think of them as soldiers, were a different matter. They did not complain, nor did they seem to notice the minor annoyances of the outdoors. Other than grunts in response to Moldor's orders, they never spoke at all. Pip had been tempted to enter their minds out of curiosity, but decided it would be an unforgiveable breach of their privacy, and doubted he would learn anything of use anyway. Moldor's mind on the other hand, was a place Pip had no desire to go. He knew all he needed to know about the man from his words and actions. He was a castle courtier, at home in the comfort of his silks and jewels, attended by a legion of servants, and no doubt quite adept at castle intrigue, but outside the castle, he was little more than a whining annoyance, worse than the buzzing insects he complained about.

"We do not visit the city," Pip said. "Because it will only delay our arrival at your land, and if things are as you say, we cannot afford delay. If I enter the city, the Council of Nobles will insist on a formal welcome, and the banquet alone could consume a day or two. We will make camp beyond the city tonight and move on at sunrise. How far beyond Gondwana is your capital?"

Moldor pouted, but he'd learned in the short journey so far that, while Pip didn't scowl like Vera, he was just as stubborn.

"Is from the Barbarian capital maybe two days or three," he said. "Was so uncomfortable I am not remembering very well."

Pip laughed. "Well, we will try to find softer spots of earth for your blanket for the next few nights, Moldor," he said. "There are no more settlements of any significance between here and the border."

"Is no need to telling me. I have traveled this way before."

Moldor continued to pout, though he mercifully kept his feelings to himself.

The following two days went quietly. As they drew nearer to the border between Barbaria and Alluria, the land became rougher, with fewer settlements, and stunted stands of gnarled trees replacing neatly tilled fields. The mountains in the distance to their front looked dark and forbidding, like some monsters hunched down waiting to pounce. Pip noticed that the four soldiers grew even quieter, not even grunting now, and their eyes never stopped roving, peering about as if

they expected something to jump at them
from behind every tree. Moldor continued to
pout, but no longer complained, and at night,
he moved his blanket as near to the fire and
Pip as possible.

Pip wanted to stay out of their minds,
because he didn't need to do that to know
what was happening. The closer the Allurians
got to home, the more a sense of fear and
dread enveloped them. That was making him
uneasy.

Finally, as they made camp the night
before crossing the border, Pip waited until
Moldor and the soldiers were settled and he
moved to where Vera sat staring into the fire.
His aide, Norbert was sleeping soundly
across from her. Tamara was nowhere to be
seen.

"Where is Tamara?" Pip asked.

"I asked her to stand guard," Vera replied.
"I do not know if you have noticed, cousin,
but the closer we get to their land, the more
nervous our companions become."

"Yes, I have noticed." Pip nodded. "That is
why I was thinking to take a gentle look into
Moldor's mind while he sleeps."

"That is a good idea, cousin, but . . .
mayhap it would be better if it was I who did
the probing."

Pip's cheeks flushed. While he was the
most powerful, it was also a fact that Vera,
having been trained in the use of her powers
since birth, was the most experienced.

Whether it was his pride, or a voice in the back of his mind that told him he must take every opportunity to improve his use of the powers with which he'd been born, he knew that he had to be the one to accomplish this task.

"I appreciate your offer, cousin," he said. "But, I think I should be able to do this. I will not go deep; only far enough to see if Moldor is leading us into some kind of trap."

Vera's look was skeptical, but she nodded.

"Very well, so shall it be. But, if you sense the slightest awareness of your presence, you must pull out immediately. If he is planning a trap, it would not be wise for him to know that we are aware of it."

Pip felt a momentary twinge of anger which quickly passed. He knew that Vera was only concerned for him. She had, after all, been his first teacher, and had saved him after Tenkuk's thugs had kidnapped him.

"Do not fear, Vera," he said. "I will withdraw at the slightest sign of awareness. Keep an eye on his men, though, in case they stir."

He also knew he didn't have to tell her that. She was already focused on the four sleeping figures.

Allowing his body to relax, Pip focused on the lanky figure stretched out beneath a blanket a few feet from where he sat. He then let his mind reach out, like tendrils of fog, and wrap around the man's head. Pip closed his eyes. At first, all he saw was a gray mist, swirling and tossing as if blown by a breeze. Then the gray mist darkened, and he saw inky blackness with flashes of red and orange. He heard muffled screams, but could make out no intelligible words. Slowly, ever so slowly, he pushed forward. The blackness seemed to thicken like treacle, not pushing back, but also not yielding. The inky darkness thickened even more, and then he bumped into something . . . a substance he didn't recognize, as hard as the rock of the mountains, but also sticky. He let the tendrils from his mind spread out, but the obstacle, whatever it was, seemed to extend in all directions. He tensed his muscles and focused harder, but as he pushed forward, he felt a slight push back, as if something behind the black barrier was reaching for him.

Suddenly, he was gripped by a sense of dread; he felt his own heart beating faster. There was something on the other side of the barrier, and it *knew* he was there. Worse, it was trying to get through the barrier to him. Holding his breath and trying to calm his beating heart, Pip quickly withdrew his probe, leaning back against Vera when he'd done so, breathing hard.

"Cousin," Vera said. "What is the matter?"

When Pip's breathing had slowed, and he felt that he had control of his voice, he looked up at Vera who was kneeling near, peering down at him with a look of concern on her face.

"I-I am not sure," he said quietly. "I could make no sense of what I saw, but there was something there."

Following his cue, Vera leaned in close and kept her voice low.

"What? You sensed something in Moldor's mind?"

"Yes, but . . . it was not Moldor," he whispered. "It was something dark, something . . . I do not know what it was, but I sense it was . . . is dangerous."

They both looked at the still sleeping Allurian. He twitched and moaned, but soon was breathing easily again.

Even with Tamara on guard, neither Pip nor Vera closed their eyes again that night.

When the sun rose the next morning, Moldor rose and stretched, again complaining about the pebbles and twigs that had disturbed his sleep. The Allurian guards rose and quietly went about preparing their morning meal. Tamara returned to the camp site, looking as if she'd slept through the night instead of patrolling around the camp to make sure no one sneaked upon them. Pip and Vera were both bleary eyed from lack of sleep, and though they tried to keep it from showing, their faces were creased with worry. Moldor did not seem to notice, but Tamara, as soon as she saw them also frowned. She said nothing, though, as they quietly ate their morning meal and then packed things in preparation for the day's journey which would take them across the border into Alluria.

When they'd packed and mounted, Moldor rode his horse near Pip. His expression was bland, but Pip could not help but wonder if the man knew of his nocturnal visit. He looked at Vera.

Let Tamara know what I learned from Moldor's mind.

Vera acknowledged his message with a barely perceptible nod, turned her horse and trotted to catch up with Tamara, who had already ridden out ahead to scout their route. This left Pip alone with the five Allurians. He did not fear that he would be able to handle them, but he was nonetheless uncomfortable in their presence, more so now that he knew that Moldor was concealing more than the identity of the demon that was plaguing Alluria.

Vera rode alongside Tamara, leaning in until the women's shoulders almost touched, for a long time. She finally pulled away and turned her horse back to where Pip rode with Moldor alongside him. Giving Pip a knowing look, she positioned her horse so that the Allurian was between them. Other than the sidelong glances he'd been giving her since the start of the journey, Moldor didn't seem to notice anything out of the ordinary.

They rode silently until they came to a

place where the earth rose upwards in a gentle slope, blocking the sight of all but the very tips of the mountains that Moldor had told them covered most of Alluria. He stopped his horse suddenly, pointing to the top of the rise.

"At top is border of Alluria," he said. "Reach top and we will be home."

There was, however, no joy in his declaration. Pip noticed that the four guards, still silent, wore even more morose expressions. His curiosity got the better of him.

"You do not seem happy to be coming home," he said.

Moldor regarded him a long time from beneath half-closed lids before answering.

"Is . . . hard to explain," he said. "I think you are not understanding."

"You might be surprised at my cousin's ability to understand strange things," Vera said from the other side of Moldor, causing him to jerk his head around. It was her longest statement to him since chiding him a few days earlier.

He smiled at her. Her return smile, Pip noted, was tight and forced.

"Why are you saying that, Lady Vera?" he asked.

"Ah, well, you see . . . my cousin has a rather checkered background. I am sure when he gets to know you better he will share it with you. He too has issues about being at home."

She shot a knowing look at Pip, causing his heart to flutter. He'd not told her about his restlessness, and surely Valdun wouldn't have mentally shared it. Oh no, he thought, it was that devilish woman's intuition that she and Zohra always talked about; that ability they had to know a man's inner thoughts, often when he himself was uncertain. He coughed and glared at her, but saw that Moldor had a look of interest on his face. Whether it was about Pip, or just the man's interest in Vera, it was a chance to get him to talk. *Hm, mayhap this woman's intuition is a useful skill after all.*

"Ah, yes," he said. "I too find myself feeling ill at ease when I return home from a journey, sad that the journey is over. Is that what you feel?"

"Yes, is so. I am feeling that I wish journey is not to end so soon. Is first time I am leaving Alluria, and is so much to see in other places."

Moldor spoke in low, almost whispering tones, glancing furtively back at the guards. They rode stoically, staring at the ground ahead of them and seemed not to have noticed.

"Mayhap, when we have taken care of the demon that plagues your land," Pip said. "You can return and see more of Pandara."

Moldor looked at Vera, a broad smile on his face for the first time.

"Yes, I am thinking I would like very much to do that." Then, his expression darkened. "But, I am thinking it will not be possible."

"Surely, your Princess Miko will allow it if we are successful against this . . . demon."

At the sound of the princess's name, Moldor shuddered and looked ahead again. His body sagged like an air bladder with a slow leak.

As Pip opened his mouth to say more, a dark shadow passed over them, and for the first time, one of the Allurian guards made a sound that wasn't a grunt. He screamed, making a high-pitched sound like a metal whistle. Pip turned, and saw the man pointing to the sky with a look of panic on his greenish face. The others, equally frightened, looked in the direction he pointed.

When Pip, Vera, and Moldor turned back in their saddles and looked up, Moldor made a mewling sound and almost fell from his saddle.

Pip and Vera began laughing as two large shapes, backlit by the sun, glided down toward them, landing softly on the slope about twenty meters away.

NINE

"D-demons," Moldor said weakly, pointing at the hulking shapes sitting placidly before them munching at the sparse vegetation.

When two shapes detached themselves from the two flying dragons and started walking toward them, Moldor's body spasmed and the four guards began whimpering liked whipped dogs.

"S-save us," Moldor pleaded. "Devour us they will."

"Oh, I don't think so," Pip said. "These are friends of mine. Hail, Draco, hail, Tyco, what brings you here?"

The larger of the two Draconians; and both were large men, clad in a leather jerkin and leather, thigh-length pants, waved at Pip.

"Hail to you, Prince Valdar," Draco said.

"We heard you were off on a quest to find a demon, and figured you might need a bit of help."

"Aye," Tyco, his companion and friend said. "And, it was boring in Draconia. Our wives and children do nothing but pester us. We were in need of some adventure."

Moldor looked from Pip to the two approaching men, his expression a study in confusion. His four guards merely looked scared.

"Herald Moldor," Pip said. "These two worthies are Draco and Tyco, warriors of Draconia, a land to the west of Barbaria. They are . . . friends of mine." He turned back to the two dragon warriors. "How did you know where to find us?"

Draco pointed behind Pip.

"We had friends to guide us," he said.

Four figures, one, large with long arms and broad shoulders, three smaller, trudged through the scattered boulders toward them. Pip recognized them even from the great distance. The shambling gait of Walu the ogre was unmistakable. The two gnomes, Gork and Gollum, were carrying their large bows, with full quivers on their backs, and Nork the troll held his ever-present wooden club, and wore a short sword at his waist.

"Have you four been following us?" Pip asked when they neared.

For all his bulk; he towered over Pip's slight form, the ogre looked shame-faced.

"Valdun order us to keep Valdar safe," he mumbled.

Pip turned and looked at Vera.

"You and Tamara were aware of this?"

Vera's ruddy complexion darkened and she looked down at the ground. Tamara came over the rise and strode quickly down to them.

"Yes, Pip," she said. "We were aware. We were told to keep it from you until we reached the border of Alluria."

"But, why?" Pip ran a hand through his flame red hair. "Why would you keep something like this from me?"

Vera laid a hand on his shoulder.

"We were only told that Hermes had seen some darkness, and that this journey to Alluria is somehow involved," she said. "There is great danger, but he could not suss the nature of that danger." She looked over at Moldor who still sat transfixed staring from the new arrivals to the grazing dragons. "Our friend here is somehow a key to this, but as you know . . . he too is unaware of the true nature of the danger. But, from his reaction to the appearance of the dragons, I think we can surmise that some dragon-like creature is involved."

Pip looked angrily at Moldor.

"Is this true, Moldor? Is the demon of Alluria a dragon?"

Moldor blinked. "I . . . am not knowing. I only know that those . . . beasts seem . . .

familiar." He looked at the new arrivals. "What manner of . . . beings are these . . . friends of yours?"

Pip introduced each, starting with Walu, the largest and most intimidating looking, although, Pip knew from experience that the gnomes, with their deadly accuracy with their bows, were probably the most dangerous. Not that it mattered to the Allurian who shrank backward from each of the Folk as they came forward to greet him. As for the Allurian soldiers, they sat in their saddles, as stiff as wooden carvings, not even their eyes moving. The gnomes found the Allurian reaction to them quite amusing—of course, Gork and Gellum found most things, including combat, amusing.

Walu walked up to Pip, his height making his head even with Pip's even astride Nightshade. He put two hairy hands on Pip's shoulders and leaned in, his shaggy forehead against Pip's.

"Long time, friend Valdar," he said in his gravelly voice. "You still practice fighting like Walu taught you?"

"Of course, old friend, although not as much as I would like."

"Mayhap Valdar too busy making baby," Gork said, causing Gellum to snort in laughter and Pip's face to darken.

"Better I think with that than with sword," Nork said, a smile creasing his narrow face.

Pip ignored their good-natured joking.

Even though he'd not known they were coming, it was good to see his old comrades once again.

"I guess you will all be coming with us to Alluria," he said, even though he had reservations about showing up with such a strange assemblage.

As if reading his mind, Vera eased her horse, Star, against Nightshade's flank so that her leg brushed against Pip's.

I have been thinking. Vera's thought came to Pip's mind. *It mayhap will not be a good idea for such a large and unusual party to arrive at the capital.*

Do you think? Pip shot back. *We are supposed to be coming to render assistance, but we will look like an invading force—especially with the dragons.*

Vera frowned at his rebuke.

There is no need for that tone. I regret that it was felt necessary to keep this from you until now. If it makes you feel any better, I objected to it. My father and Hermes overruled me. Now, I have a plan if you are of a mind to listen.

Pip realized that Vera would never lie to him, and he believed that she would have supported him. He was confused, and somewhat disappointed, that Valdun and Hermes felt that he had to be treated thus, but there was naught he could do about it in their present circumstance. He mentally nodded to Vera to explain her plan.

The plan was simple, and he chided himself for letting his pique at being kept in the dark so long keep him from immediately thinking of it. He, Vera and Tamara would wipe all memories of the encounter with the Draconian and the Folk from the minds of Moldor and the four Allurian guards. The dragon warriors and the Folk would, in turn, conceal themselves to avoid anyone of Alluria seeing them unless absolutely necessary. Pip, Vera, Tamara, and Norbert—who had served Pip long enough that he was no longer shocked, or even surprised at the strange things that seemed to happen where Pip was involved—would continue on with their Allurian escorts as if nothing had happened.

The only part of the plan that worried Pip was the presence of the two dragons. They'd triggered some emotional reaction in Moldor and the guards, and if the demon was indeed related to dragons, their use in helping Alluria could present a serious problem. Draco assured him, however, that he and Tyco would keep the dragons out of sight, and the creatures, now that Draconia was no longer at war, were really quite docile. Each of them, though, was as big as three oxen, and looking into their gaping maw, Pip found it hard to apply the word docile to them. He did, however, trust the dragon warriors as men of honor, so he bid them on their way. The Folk faded into the rocky hills like morning mist under the searing rays of the sun, and once they were again alone, Pip suggested they be on their way.

"Yes, is good idea to go," Moldor said. He looked up at the sky, a momentary look of worry creasing his forehead. Then, he smiled. "We will be at castle by nightfall. Will be big banquet to welcome you."

Charles Ray

TEN

Pip had thought Barbaria a bleak country, with its rundown farms and drably-dressed inhabitants, but Alluria made Pandara's neighbor look like paradise.

The settlements, sparsely populated at best, were spread thinly across the bleak landscape. There was more flat land than had first seemed likely, but it was rocky and covered with stunted trees and rough grass that the even the Allurian mounts ate only reluctantly. There was at least the advantage of sufficient water. Many streams poured out of the nearby mountains, cutting ragged scars across the land, and forcing them to spend time finding places to cross.

The few people they encountered, some

greenish of complexion like Moldor, some of a pale reddish hue, weren't hostile, but nor were they friendly. They bent to their tasks of tilling the hard earth or tending their stunted cattle, sheep or goats, ignoring the travelers as they passed.

Pip hoped the Folk and the dragon warriors were keeping well out of sight. After seeing the reaction Moldor and his men had to the sight of the two dragons, he could only imagine the panic that they would generate in the general populace.

Even the sky, leaden gray, seemed unfriendly.

Added to this was the sense of unease that had draped itself over Pip since his visit into Moldor's dark mind.

Since discovering his powers, he'd entered the consciousness of several creatures, including a hawk that had helped him during one of his missions against Tenkuk, but had finally gone back to the wild. He had even entered the mind of the monster, Tenkuk, albeit briefly. But, he'd never been in a mind that gave off nothing but darkness the likes of which he'd sensed inside Moldor. He'd toyed with the idea of probing the soldiers, or getting Vera to do it, but decided to wait until he knew more about the land they were entering. Not the best military strategy, this he knew. Better to know before you go, but they were in it now, and it seemed better not to take further chances. Minds that could cloak themselves the way Moldor's mind seemed to be cloak, might not be easy to penetrate. The way Moldor had been twitching just as Pip withdrew could have been an indication that he knew he was being probed—Pip could not tell, and the man hadn't shown any signs of suspicion since—but, he would take no chances. He was confident that he and his comrades could handle whatever Alluria could throw at them.

His first sight of the castle that sat on a hill overlooking a valley that was nestled in the shadow of the surrounding jagged peaks caused him a moment of doubt about the ability to *handle* Alluria's problems. A dark, hulking structure, it seemed to be poised to pounce on those in the valley below. It was more ominous looking than Tenkuk's dark castle had been. For one thing, it was more of a fortress than even that evil man's had been, high black stone walls with round turrets at each corner, it looked as if it had been built to withstand a siege.

The impression was no better as they approached the main gate. More than twenty feet high and ten wide, it was made of thick planks reinforced with metal bars. And, unlike Daphne's castle whose gates were always open to her subjects, the gates to the castle of Alluria were closed, and guarded by armored men carrying crossbows who stood menacingly in the towers on the wall at the sides of the gate.

"Who goes there?" one of the guards shouted down to them as they approached the edge of the moat that surrounded the structure.

"Is Royal Herald Moldor, returning with friends . . . at command of Her Highness, Princess Miko."

"What is password?" the gruff voiced man said.

Moldor looked confused, and then he snapped his fingers.

"Three Blind Mice," he said.

The guard turned and waved at someone Pip couldn't see. There was a rumbling sound, and the heavy gate began to lower toward them.

"Do they not know you?" he said to Moldor.

Moldor shrugged.

"Is way with guards," he said. "Is jealousy because I work in main part of castle. Is no problem."

Without waiting for a response from Pip, Moldor kicked his horse forward and stepped onto the gate, now serving as a bridge across the moat. The four guards fell in behind him, their horses' hooves making a clattering sound on the planks.

"Well, I imagine we are to follow them," Pip said to his three startled-looking companions. "Welcome to Alluria."

Nightshade snorted derisively as Pip urged

him onto the bridge.

Not a very welcoming place.

Pip had no retort to his horse's observation. As they passed under the archway into the castle's front courtyard, Pip looked up. The guards on the battlements above them kept their crossbows at the ready, not exactly aimed at the riders below, but not so far away that it would take more than a heartbeat to bring them to bear. On the hard packed earth that covered the courtyard, armed guards flanked the path from the gate to a large raised patio attached to the front of the main castle building. These soldiers were armed with long spears which they gripped tightly as Pip and the others rode past.

Moldor and the Allurian soldiers came to a stop at the bottom step of the patio, dismounted, and then moved to the right, standing at rigid attention. Even their horses stood silent, not even their tails twitching.

As Pip dismounted, his sense of anxiety soared. There was something—many things—about this place that just seemed . . . wrong. Vera, Tamara, and Norbert dismounted and stood beside him. Vera and Tamara flanked Pip, Vera to his left, their heads constantly moving to take in the entire courtyard, their hands not far from the swords at their waists. Norbert moved up beside Vera, his hand also on his sword, his young face drawn and pale.

"Why do we wait here?" Vera whispered.

"Mayhap for the princess to grant us an audience," Pip answered quietly.

"My father would never keep visitors waiting like this," she said.

"Yes, Valdun is a kind king. My Aunt Daphne would also not keep people waiting, not even the lowliest commoner. But, not all leaders are the same, as you well know."

"Well, I for one do not think much of Alluria."

"Sh, remember, cousin, we are their guests. We must not forget our manners--"

"Even if they have none," Vera finished for him.

Pip could not suppress a chuckle, which earned him a harsh look from Moldor.

"Is forbidden to speak until princess arrives," he said in a quiet voice. "Is stiff punishment for speaking."

Pip stared at the man, thinking he must surely be joking, but the stern set of his lip, and the fear in his yellow eyes said otherwise. Alluria was getting stranger, and more annoying by the minute. He wanted to get away from the dull routine of Lands End and have adventure, but this was not what he'd had in mind. He began wondering what Zohra was doing at that moment; probably just sitting down to evening meal with his aunt. The thought made him feel warm inside. He smiled back at Moldor. The man's eyes went wide in surprise.

There was a stirring in the courtyard; not a sound really, more a feeling of sound, as the soldiers, already standing at attention, stiffened even further. Moldor's back seemed to have had an iron rod affixed to it. He stood so stiffly erect his body quivered.

There was a creaking sound. Pip looked up and saw the large double doors at the back of the raised patio begin to swing outwards. They were being pushed by two young men in tight fitting black tunics and knee-length trousers, who kept their heads and backs bent as they pushed.

When the doors were fully opened, the two men scurried behind them, waiting, Pip assumed, to be told to close them once again.

He looked at the dark, gaping maw that was the door. A shadow of something moved, and the tallest man Pip had ever seen walked through the door and onto the patio.

The top of the door was at least eight feet from the floor, and the man's bald head nearly brushed it as he came through. Though tall, he was stick thin, with sloping shoulders beneath the voluminous robe he wore. His skin was the color of chalk, with the texture of wind-scoured rocks. He had a long, narrow nose with large round eyes set close on either side. The nose plunged straight down to a dark, brown mustache that drooped to either side of razor-thin lips that were set in a look of derision. His light blue eyes scanned the crowd in the courtyard the way a vulture scans the terrain for carrion, settling for a long time on Pip before moving on. The man's scrutiny sent shivers down Pip's spine.

The man walked to the edge of the patio, standing directly in front of Pip, his glare slicing through him like an arrow.

"Who comes beseeching an audience of her Celestial Highness?" he asked in a booming voice that was out of character with his emaciated, corpse-like frame.

Moldor, quivering like an aspen in a spring windstorm, shuffled forward and turned to face the man.

"Is Moldor the Royal Herald," he said in a weak voice. "Have come to ask Beneficent One to ask Her Highness to grant audience to unworthy self."

Pip had heard similar rituals before in Barbaria. Such wastes of time were never allowed in Pandara or the Land of Fire, nor did the people of Avia or Draconia resort to such verbal circumlocutions when a meeting was sought with their leaders. Pip had come to the conclusion that the elaborateness was directly proportional to the lack of substance that would come out of any such meeting. He pressed his lips tightly to avoid inadvertently tittering, or making some comment that would likely mortally offend their host,

"And, why does the weasel, Moldor, seek the assistance of Larok, advisor to Her

Celestial Highness?"

So, Pip thought, this was Galen's counterpart. His old teacher would never play such foolish word games; Queen Daphne would never allow it in the first place. Surely, as the princess's advisor, he *must* know of Moldor's mission, and therefore, know why he sought an audience. Pip blew a breath out slowly, but his body thrummed with agitation. The snide expression on Larok's ashen face indicated that this senseless ritual could go on for some time.

Moldor bowed low, bent at the waist as he'd done before Queen Daphne.

"Unworthy one has completed mission assigned," he said. "Have visit demesne of Pandara where queen has agreed to send mighty warrior to help Alluria in time of need."

Larok sniffed loudly and looked derisively at the obsequious minion.

"And, who is this mighty warrior?"

Pip was unsure of the proper protocol, but he bridled at Moldor's calling Pandara a demesne. He stepped forward, looking up at Larok.

"I am Prince Valdar from the *Kingdom* of Pandara," he said. "Her Majesty, Queen Daphne, has ordered me to render assistance to--"

Larok held a hand up, not looking at Pip, but at Moldor.

"Who is this child, and who has given him

leave to speak?" His voice echoed off the stone walls.

"Uh, forgive him, honorable one," Moldor said. His voice quivered. "He is not knowing ways of Alluria."

"Then, I advise you in the strongest terms to teach him the ways before he speaks out of turn again, or it will go badly for both of you."

Pip started forward, but Vera laid a hand on his arm, just a light pressure, but it stopped him.

Do not provoke him, cousin. I sense that this is a dangerous man.

As do I, but I cannot stand by and allow him to insult my queen as he is doing.

Do not forget, Pip; we are guests here. Let us see what he is about before we decide what to do.

Pip took a deep breath. As usual, Vera's wisdom was impeccable. He looked around. It was not that the three of them, four counting young Norbert, who was as red-faced as Pip, couldn't acquit themselves against even the number of armed soldiers in the courtyard— and, he sensed the dragon warriors and the Folk nearby—but, it would not be proper to engage in conflict with people who had asked for their aid, even if their manners were lacking. He took a step backwards, and moved his hand away from the hilt of his sword.

The cadaverous specter standing on the patio looked down at him and grinned, a lecherous contortion of his lips.

"That is more like it," Larok said. "Lesser beings must always understand their place."

Pip heard a snarling sound in his head, unsure whether it had come from Vera or Tamara, but he knew the two women were having as much difficulty restraining themselves as he was. Even Nightshade, standing behind him, snorted and pawed at the flagstones of the courtyard. He could feel the waves of anger emanating from the black stallion.

"Now, Moldor," Larok continued. "You wish me to believe that this stripling, the even weaker looking male behind him, and two females are the warriors the . . . queen of Pandara has sent to help us in our hour of need?"

"I-I w-was assured, noble one, that he is being the best warrior the de-, kingdom had to offer."

Larok played with the ends of his mustache as he looked at Pip, his expression similar to a farmer looking over a cow he was considering buying.

"So, scrawny one," he said. "You are the best warrior your little . . . kingdom has to offer, eh? Her Highness will be sorely disappointed when she sets eyes on you and your motley crew."

Pip drew himself to his full height, locking gaze with the insufferable popinjay. He took a deep breath to keep his voice from cracking.

"I can assure you that the four of us have experience in warfare," he said. "While I do not know the nature of the threat to Alluria, I doubt that it is much worse than that which we have already faced . . . and vanquished."

"My, my, strong words from one so small, Valdar . . . such a strong name, too, for one such as you."

"That name was given to me by my father and mother, Larok--"

Larok's lips curved downward, and his eyes blazed.

"That is Honorable Larok to you, boy!"

"As you wish, Honorable Larok," Pip said. "And, I am *Prince* Valdar to you."

Larok clenched his fists and pursed his thin lips.

"Of course, *Prince* Valdar," he said. "But, before I present you to Her Highness, I would like a . . . demonstration of your abilities. Would that be amenable to you?"

Anger coursed through Pip. The Allurians asked for help, and now this fool wanted him to fight the people seeking help. He could feel the heat rising in his cheeks. Fine, if he wanted a demonstration, Pip would give him one.

"It would, *Honorable* Larok," he said. "Pick your best warrior and I will best him in whatever form of combat you choose."

"Ah, no, my young friend, not merely one warrior. If you wish to demonstrate your skills, I would have you fight against four of

Alluria's best."

Pip was now beginning to feel the blood heat of battle.

"As you wish," he said. "Bring them on."

Do not use your full power, Pip, Vera warned. *There is no sense in letting him know all that you can do.*

Do not worry, I will not hurt them, just pummel them a bit.

He turned and smiled at Vera. She dipped her head a fraction and returned his smile.

I will keep an eye out, just in case they do not fight fair, she said.

As will I, Tamara chimed in.

This, Pip thought, should prove interesting.

"How do you wish me to fight your chosen warriors?" Pip asked Larok.

"Oh, I believe my warriors will use their spears. Have you any objections?"

Pip unsheathed his short sword.

"None at all," he said.

Larok pointed at four of the largest warriors lining the path from the gate. He said something in a language that Pip did not understand, and the four stepped forward, forming a line, their spears angled upwards.

Pip turned and faced him, holding his sword low at his side. He looked from left to right. The warriors returned his gaze with feral grins, and began advancing toward him, lowering their spears so that the razor sharp points aimed at his chest. He was pretty sure by that action that the words he hadn't understood were that they were to attempt to seriously injure, if not kill, him. So be it, he thought. Let them try. He calmed his breathing, focusing his energy for what lay ahead, and waited for them to close the gap.

The second man from Pip's left advanced a step further than the other three. He snarled. "Honor of first blood is being mine," he said, and thrust his spear forward.

The blade entered the space that would have been occupied by Pip's chest, except that at the moment before it did, he flickered and shifted to a position behind and the thrusting warrior's right shoulder. He raised his sword and brought it down, knob of the hilt first, to the base of the man's skull, sending a jolt of energy through it as he did. The man slumped forward. Before his limp body hit the flagstones, Pip swung his sword hilt to the right, striking the man there in the temple, and sending a smaller jolt of energy. The man's eyes rolled back in their sockets and he sagged down to fall face down next to his unconscious comrade.

The remaining two soldiers, momentarily stunned at the speed of Pip's handling their friends, leveled their spears and started turning back toward him. Before they could get set, Pip leapt high in the air, landing with his left foot on the left hand of one, and his right foot on the right hand of the other. He sent a shock through both feet, causing them to loosen their grip on their spears. The useless weapons clattered to the cobblestones. Pip whipped his hand to the right, slamming the man there in the temple, and as he crumpled, he spun the sword and placed the point at the throat of the last standing warrior, pushing just hard enough to break the skin and cause a drop of blood to well up.

"Yield or die," he said.

"Urp," the warrior said.

"Do you yield?" Pip asked.

The man's strained to look down at the sword beneath his chin. His Adam's apple bobbed up and down.

"Urp," he said. "I y-yield, sire."

Pip pulled his sword back, wiped the blade on the shoulder of the man's tunic and slid it back into the sheath. Casually, he turned his back on the pale, panting soldier and looked up at Larok, throwing his head and shoulders back.

"Well, Larok," he said. "If these four are the best you have, I can see why you need my assistance."

Show off, Vera shot at him. *You fought well, but the theatrics were unnecessary.*

That, my dear cousin, is the only thing these idiots understand, Pip shot back.

Larok stood glaring down at him, his face a stunning mixture of emotions. His brow furrowed in worry, his eyes were wide in amazement, and his thin lips curled downward in an angry snarl. A line of spittle dribbled from the side of his mouth. He clenched his fists at his side.

"Well played, Prince Valdar," a sultry female voice said from the darkness beyond the doors. "It pleases me to see someone beat my advisor at his childish games."

Larok's mouth dropped open. The standing warriors all dropped to the flagstones, prostrating themselves, as did Moldor. Pip could only stand and stare.

Through the door walked a creature like no other he'd ever seen in his short life.

ELEVEN

Pip surmised from the reaction of the Allurians in the courtyard—excepting Larok, of course—that the stunning female emerging from the shadows and walking toward the front of the patio was the Princess Miko.

She had the face of a child, a petulant child, but even younger than Pip. Oval eyes that shone green and sparkled in the light of the flickering torches set in the stone walls of the courtyard, and highlighted by dark makeup that accented her long, dark lashes, that fluttered as she glanced around. She was slight of build, with small breasts sheathed in a halter made of spun gold. Her midriff was bare to just below her navel. Her waist was small, flaring out into the beginnings of womanly hips encased in gossamer pantaloons that also displayed shapely legs. On her small feet she wore golden slippers. As she walked to the edge of the patio, she seemed to glide across the stones.

She stopped at the edge, small hands on her hips, and smiled down at Pip.

He felt his breath catch in his throat, and a warm glow in his chest as he looked up at her. But, along with the warm glow, he felt a warning buzz in his head. He gazed into her eyes and saw . . . nothing. The green orbs looking back at him lacked the glimmer of life, as if she was a mobile statue carved from a block of ivory. Yet, he still felt drawn to her.

Vera's voice in his mind pulled at him and he felt as if he was awakening from a restless sleep.

Take care, cousin, there is something amiss about this one.

What is it, Vera?

I do not know. I tried to probe her, but encountered only blackness.

But, she is so beautiful.

So is the rock snake of the Great Desert, but that beauty conceals deadly venom.

Miko's gaze shifted from Pip to Vera and a frown creased her brow. Her eyes seemed to glaze over. She turned back to Pip, a mirthless smile on her carmine lips.

"So, Prince Valdar of Pandara," she said. "You have proven yourself as a worthy warrior. I would speak with you so that you will know what services I require."

Pip lowered his gaze, letting his head droop forward in a sketchy bow. He took a deep breath to regain his equilibrium, Vera's warning firm in his mind.

"As you wish, Your Highness," he said when he looked back up at her.

She lifted a hand and beckoned him to step up onto the patio.

"Come, then. We will converse in my chambers." When Vera, Tamara, and Norbert stepped forward with him, she held a hand up. "I wish to speak with Prince Valdar privately. The rest of you will be shown to your chambers. We will join you later for a welcome banquet in the main hall."

I do not like this, Vera said.

Do not worry, cousin, she is only a girl. If I can handle four warriors, she should pose no real danger.

I sense something strong in her, stronger than any warrior I have ever encountered.

Come now, Vera, surely you do not think I am unable to handle this?

Vera frowned deeply. *Very well. Just be careful.*

Am I not always careful?

She did not reply, but Pip saw doubt clearly on her face. With a bit of trepidation, he mounted the steps to the patio to stand beside Miko. Up close she was a full hand shorter than he, but the lifelessness in her gaze was even more pronounced, and he could feel a wave of energy emanating from her like the heat from Auric's forge. It gave him a prickly feeling throughout his body. He fought the urge to scratch. He would not give Vera the pleasure of seeing how nervous he was.

Taking his hand, Miko led him into the castle. Her hand in his, despite the coldness in her eyes, was warm and soft, and he felt a stirring in his loins that reminded him of . . . Zohra. At the thought of his pregnant wife waiting for him back in Lands End, some of the warmth receded.

They walked silently through the great room behind the entrance door, through a slit in great drapes that hung from the vaulted ceiling, and into a long hallway lit by many torches in sconces along both sides, until she stopped in front of a normal sized door. She pushed the door open and stepped aside, motioning him to enter.

"No, Your Highness," he said. "It would not be appropriate for me to precede you."

She smiled, and he saw a flicker of something that was almost warmth in her green eyes.

"Not only are you a great warrior, but a gallant as well," she said. Her body brushed against him as she entered the room. "Please, Valdar . . . may I call you by your name? You must call me Miko. Please, make yourself comfortable. Would you like some refreshment?"

When Pip stepped across the threshold his breath caught in his throat. Accustomed as he was to the simplicity of the amphitheater where Valdun had his hut and the understated elegance of Daphne's bedchamber, the sight of Miko's chamber stunned him. The walls were covered with shiny, lavender cloth that hung in folds from ceiling to floor, the floor covered in dark, brown wool that his feet sank into up to the ankles, and on six large tables scattered around the room was a king's ransom in gold, silver and sparkling gems, haphazardly spread about like children's toys. At the far side of the room was a large, canopied bed with black, silken coverings and canopy, large enough to accommodate four people the size of Walu the ogre. Next to the bed stood an ornate table carved of a dark brown wood. On the table were a silver urn, two gold flagons, and a silver tray laden with strange looking fruits. Two stools made of the same wood as the table were arranged across from each other. It was as if Miko had been expecting to entertain him. His senses went to full alert, but he didn't want to alarm or alert her—which he was not sure.

"I did not think you meant that we would meet in your . . . bedchamber, Prin-, Miko," he said.

She twirled around, waving her arms and pointing at things at random.

"How better to get to know each other," she said.

"Uh, yes, I suppose you are correct." He made his way to the table, stopping at the stool nearest the door and waited for her to sit.

She pouted at him.

"For a warrior you are certainly acting ill at ease," she said. "One would think you would be more forward, alone in a chamber with a defenseless female." She batted her long lashes at him, and pulled a strand of hair to her lips.

"It is . . . uh, in Pandara, it is not appropriate for a man to be alone in a bedchamber with a woman not his kin."

She sat, crossing her legs and leaned forward until her small breasts pressed against the table.

"So, you have not had much experience with women then?"

"Your Highness, I am married, and will soon be a father."

She laughed, this time Pip saw that she was truly amused, but of what he could not fathom.

"You did not answer my question, Valdar. I would guess that you married the first and only woman that you have ever had. That does not count as much experience."

The way she lowered the timber of her voice when she spoke, and the way she stretched her shoulders to thrust out her breasts, made Pip uncomfortable. His clothing felt much too tight, and there was tightness in his chest. She was right in what she'd said; he really had very little experience with women. Zohra had been the first for him—and only, he reminded himself. He steeled himself against whatever Miko was using to throw him so off balance, setting up the defenses Hermes had taught him.

"That does not matter, Your Highness," he said. "We are here to discuss business. Your herald said that your . . . kingdom was plagued by a demon that your army has been unable to vanquish. If I am to serve you in that capacity, I must know as much as possible about this . . . demon."

Ignoring him, Miko lifted the urn and poured a thick amber liquid into the two flagons. She pushed one across to Pip.

"Very well, if you must. I did not know that you Pandarans were so standoffish. Had I known I might have had Moldor ask for help from the Barbarians; they at least are a livelier lot. Please, drink. This is a special brew of our people, made from the honey flower. It has special . . . regenerative powers." Her smile was wolfish.

Two can play at that game, Pip thought. I will not let myself be led into a trap. He pushed the flagon to the side.

"What is the nature of this demon, and where can it be found?"

Miko's hands tightened around her flagon,

and her eyes blazed. Pip smiled inwardly. *So, you do not like it when someone refuses to play your game. Vera would be proud of me. But, Zohra must never know of this—even though nothing is happening, nothing will happen—she would not understand.*

"Yes, the demon. I know not all of its powers. Only that it is very powerful—it destroyed, or mayhap ate, ten of my warriors, and it has killed much livestock on the holdings near its lair. It has a lair somewhere in the Mountain of the Dark Spirits to the south of here."

"What does this demon look like?"

Her eyes shifted away from his face.

"What does it look like? What does that matter? It is a demon. I suppose it is ugly and has large teeth and claws."

Pip knew instantly that she lied. She knew more than she was willing to tell. He sent a gentle probe her way, but met right away with a dark hardness through which he could not break. He sensed no resistance, just an immovable object, and she did not seem to have noticed his attempt.

"It matters," he said. "Because, if I am to fight this thing, it is helpful to know as much about it as possible. Going blind against an enemy is dangerous." *I am one to talk,* Pip thought. *I think mayhap you are not an ally, and I came here knowing nothing about you.*

"Yes, I see your point. I am sorry, though, that I cannot be of more help with what the beast looks like. I can tell you that it is dangerous, and that you must kill it immediately when you encounter it."

She had said beast. It might have been a mere figure of speech, but in Pip's experience, when people said *beast*, they referred to an animal, and if the demon was a dragon, to most it would be thought of as a particularly monstrous animal. That would explain the reaction to the dragon warriors. If the demon turned out to be a dragon, there might be a way to reason with it, Pip thought. Dragons were incredibly ancient creatures, older even than the fairies, and were not evil by nature. They were rumored to be intelligent, but were often demonized because of their appearance. Having been bedeviled by others from childhood because his red hair and reddish skin marked him apart from others in Lands End, Pip understood the pain of such behavior. He would not be guilty of such.

"I think it best to first try and reason with it," he said. "Mayhap there is a reason it is attacking Alluria, and if we determine what that reason is, we can stop the trouble."

For the first time, Pip saw something akin to true emotion in Miko's expression. Her face paled and her eyes became round like the saucers stacked near the tray of fruit. Her body went rigid.

"No," she almost shouted. "You must kill it!"

"But, why not try to find out what it

wants?"

"I know what it wants. It wants to kill me."

"I thought you knew nothing about this demon?"

"You are right," she said. "There is one thing I know that I did not tell you. This . . . demon . . . killed my twin sister, Miyako. Three months ago, it took her from her bedchamber. So, you understand; there is no reasoning with it. You must find it, and you must *kill* it."

TWELVE

Though not totally convinced, Pip felt that he did understand somewhat why Miko held the feeling she did, and maybe even why she seemed to be so consumed by the blackness which he could neither penetrate nor understand. If he'd had a sister or brother, and someone or some*thing* had . . . well, he too would be consumed with grief and rage. After swearing that he would kill the demon as soon as he met it, Miko returned to her normal, cold-eyed, flirtatious demeanor, and asked Pip to escort her to the main hall for the celebratory dinner.

"My people have been preparing it since the sun appeared this day," she said. "We must not disappoint them."

She led him back the way they'd come,

but the great hall they entered was a far cry from what it had been when Pip first saw it. Round tables with sparkling white linen covers were dotted about the room. Eight chairs were at each table, and in the center of each was a large bowl of the same thick amber drink Miko had had in her room. At the far wall, in front of a large red banner featuring a black bear holding a spear in its paw, was a round table, twice as large as the others, set similarly, at which sat Vera, Tamara, Norbert, Larok and Moldor. There were three empty chairs. Miko led Pip toward that table. People at the other tables, Pip assumed them to be Allurian nobles and their wives, stood and bowed low as they passed.

"I assume we are bound for the head table," he said. "But, I see three empty chairs. Are we expecting another guest?"

"The empty chair is in honor of my sister, Miyako," Miko said, without breaking stride.

When they arrived at the table, everyone stood. Moldor bowed low. Larok inclined his head slightly, staring at Pip through narrowed eyes. Vera looked at Pip with her eyebrows raised. He smiled and shook his head.

Miko took her time seating herself, and then nodded for everyone else to take their seats. A servant scurried to her side with a golden flagon, not of the amber liquid, but of a thick red drink that looked suspiciously like blood to Pip.

Miko stood and raised her flagon.

"I would like to propose a toast to our new friends, Prince Valdar of Pandara and his companions," she said. "To their success in riding Alluria of a most worrisome . . . problem."

She lifted her flagon to her lips, turning her head so that she could look at Pip over the rim. He lifted a flagon of the amber liquid and held it to his lips, but did not swallow.

"You do not like our honey wine, Prince Valdar?" Larok said.

"I do not take strong drink, Larok," Pip said. *And, I strongly advise the two of you to avoid it as well,* he thought at Vera and Tamara.

Norbert, whose flagon was halfway to his lips when he saw that Pip wasn't drinking, copied him and put his flagon back on the table.

"It is forbidden for a Pandaran soldier to drink spirits when on duty," he said. "And, as aide-de-camp to Prince Valdar, I am always on duty."

"You Pandarans are a strange lot," Larok said. He sniffed and plucked at his mustache. "Allurian warriors can hold their drink and still fight all day."

Pip wanted to say that if the performance of the four he'd defeated was an example of what the Allurian army could do, they should consider becoming teetotalers. What he said instead was, "Each to his own. In Pandara, each soldier is given great responsibility. It is easier to carry out that responsibility with a clear head. When off duty, our soldiers have been known to imbibe quite freely."

Miko's advisor took a long drink, wiped flecks of foam from his mustache, and laughed. "When will you be off duty, young prince?"

"When we have completed the mission."

"Well, I look forward to the completion of your mission, Prince. Mayhap we can have another contest then, to see if you can drink as well as you fight."

"Princess Miko said the demon is in the Mountain of Dark Spirits," Pip said. "What can you tell me about them?"

"Not much I'm afraid. The mountain is in a part of Alluria that is not, how you say, friendly to life. There are no farms, and even the hunters avoid it."

"Well, that would make sense as a place for a demon to live, but if this is a place that you do not go, how do you know the demon lives there?"

Larok's eyes did a little dance. He looked down at his drink. Miko had done the same just as she was about to lie.

"We started hearing reports of cattle missing near the mountain," Larok said. "Then, we sent a group of soldiers into the area to check, and they never returned."

"How long has this demon been a

problem?"

Larok played with the ends of his mustache, still avoiding looking Pip in the eye.

"Six months, mayhap a year," he said.

And, Pip thought, the lies just keep piling higher and higher.

Pip finally gave up trying to get the truth from anyone. Miko and Larok just continued to tell lie after lie, often contradicting each other or themselves. He considered pointing this out, but decided it would gain him nothing, and would alert them that he knew they were up to something. Moldor remained silent during the entire meal, responding to each of Pip's questions with, "I am knowing nothing." The food, consisting of large portions of beef that had been roasted dark brown, unleavened bread, and some unfamiliar vegetables, was good. Pip and his colleagues washed their food down with water, reckoning that they'd be able to smell or taste any poisons in it.

He was relieved when, after several hours of desultory conversation, Princess Miko declared that she was bored and was going to sleep. Without ceremony or fanfare, she simply stood, yawned, announced that she was leaving, and departed. Within minutes of her departure, the great hall was empty of guests.

Moldor guided them to their chambers, located in an area of the palace remote from

Miko's chambers, much to Pip's relief. While he'd been successful in resisting her thus far, he didn't want to have to fend off a late night visit. Luckily, Norbert had been assigned an anteroom of the chambers assigned to him, and Vera and Tamara were together in an adjacent chamber.

After bidding them a good sleep, Moldor left.

"Sleep well," Pip said to the others. "We leave at cock's crow."

"Yes, we will need every ounce of our energy if we are to kill a demon," Tamara said.

Pip hesitated in the doorway.

"About that," he said. "Miko was insistent that we kill the demon immediately upon encountering it. But, I have a feeling that all is not as it seems."

"Cousin, are you saying that you will not kill this thing?" Vera asked.

Pip shook his head.

"I am not saying anything until I know more," he said. "I might not be female, but I too have intuition; and my . . . intuition tells me that something here in Alluria is very wrong."

THIRTEEN

Pip was awake and dressed the next morning long before the sun made its appearance in the east. He roused Norbert, Vera and Tamara, and the four of them went to the castle kitchen where a sleepy cook gave them meat and bread left over from the banquet, which they washed down with a strong, brown brew that the cook said was made from the crushed beans of a plant that grew in the hills to the east.

They'd saddled their horses and were about to mount when Larok, with a bleary looking Moldor in tow, approached them.

"You leave early, Prince Valdar," Larok said. "I beseech you; please wait until Moldor here can get a horse."

"I do not believe taking him along is a

good idea," Pip said. "He is not a warrior, and I would not want to be responsible for harm befalling him."

Larok's face hardened.

"I really must insist. Moldor is not a warrior, that much is true, but he can guide you directly to the Mountain of Dark Spirits. This will save you much time if you do not have to search for it."

"Mayhap the Pandaran is right," Moldor said, squirming under Larok's relentless glare. "I am not being of much help."

"Silence, toad," Larok said. "It has been decided. You will accompany them." He turned to go, stopped and whirled around, pinning the quivering herald with a withering glare. "And, need I remind you what the penalty for failure is?"

Moldor cringed, holding his hands up in supplication.

"N-no, esteemed one, I w-will not f-fail."

"See that you do not." With that, Larok spun on his heels and strode off.

Pip looked at Vera who shrugged.

"Very well," he said. "Moldor, get your mount and whatever equipment and supplies you will need. We depart as soon as you are ready."

Still shaking, Moldor ducked his head and scurried off in the direction of the stables.

"I do not like this," Vera said.

"Larok is sending Moldor to spy upon us," Tamara said.

"I know this," Pip said. "But, at least, this way we know the identity of the spy, and can keep an eye on him."

"Let us hope that spying is all that he is charged with doing," Vera said. "If he tries anything else, I will personally skewer him."

"And, I will roast him like a haunch of goat," Tamara said.

Pip thought that it was a good thing the herald hadn't overheard the conversation. Clearly the man feared Larok, but he'd never faced the fury of Vera and Tamara. Pip had seen it, though, when they'd rescued him from Tenkuk's soldiers. If Moldor crossed either woman, he would pray for Larok's punishment to replace what they would do to him.

They waited impatiently for nearly an hour for Moldor to return. When he did, his mood was still dour. He led a splay-legged gray horse that looked as unhappy as he did at the prospect of venturing into the wilds with Pip and his crew.

"Are you ready to depart, Moldor?" Pip asked.

The man's eyes glistened with unshed tears.

"Am having no choice," he said.

"Well, mount up. We have a long journey ahead of us."

Without waiting for a response, Pip swung up onto Nightshade's back and urged the black stallion forward. The rest mounted and followed; Moldor followed along behind, his head sunk into his chest.

Pip let Nightshade follow a trail of his own choosing, knowing that the animal knew better than anyone where they were heading. He could feel the quivering of the horse's flanks. Nightshade was a war horse, and was looking forward to the adventure. Pip only wished that he shared the sense of anticipation.

Only a few miles from Miko's castle, the land changed—and not for the better. Scattered farms petered out to nothing but barren landscape populated by stunted trees and large boulders with the dark mountains as a backdrop. Their destination, the Mountain of Dark Spirits, looked appropriately named. A large, black pyramid-shaped peak with serrated edges, it looked like a dragon hunched over on the ground waiting to pounce upon unwary travelers. The only signs of life were huge birds, carrion eaters from the looks of them, perched in the tops of the trees or soared in great circles in the blue-gray, cloudless sky. The only sounds, aside from the clop of their horses' hooves on the hard, gray earth, was the moan of wind blowing across the barren land.

Pip sat silently astride his horse for an hour after the last sign of human habitation, and then he signaled Nightshade to stop, holding a hand up to halt the others.

"W-why are we stopping?" Moldor asked.

"We are still having more than a day before we are reaching the mountain."

"I think it is time for me to introduce you to the rest of my party," Pip said.

Moldor looked confused. Vera shot Pip a warning glance. *Are you sure this is a good idea?*

Yes. If he will be with us when we encounter the monster, he needs to know who we are.

She shrugged as if to say the decision was his to make, but she did not agree. So be it, Pip thought. As commander, the responsibility of failure is mine alone. He sent a silent signal summoning those he knew were shadowing them.

"W-what are you m-meaning, the r-rest of your p-party," the befuddled Moldor asked.

His question was answered by two large shadows that zipped over him, followed by the sound of footsteps scrabbling over the hard earth to their right. When he looked up, he made a sound like a small rodent. His horse screamed and reared on its hind legs, sending him tumbling over its haunches. He landed on his back on the hard ground, momentarily stunned. When he could breathe again, he curled into a fetal position, whining like a whipped dog.

The two dragons landed gently ten feet in front of them. Walu, Nork, Gork, and Gellum trotted up, coming to a stop near the still whimpering Moldor.

"P-please," he said. "N-not let them to h-hurt me." He covered his head with his hands.

"What little man cry about?" Nork asked.

"I think your sudden arrival shocked him." Pip chuckled. "Or, mayhap he is afraid of the dragons."

Despite her misgivings about exposing the others to Moldor, Vera also laughed at his pathetic figure.

"Or mayhap it is that you are so ugly," she said.

"Maybe Walu ugly because he so big," Nork said. "But, Nork most handsome of the Folk—everybody know that."

"Almost as handsome as us," Gork and Gellum said in unison.

"Uh, not need to be handsome when great warrior like me," Walu said, waving his huge fists in front of Nork's face.

"Okay, okay, let us all calm down," Pip said. "Moldor, get up. These are our friends; they will not harm you."

Moldor had been focusing on the dragons, but when he turned and saw Walu looming over him, his mouth gaped open and he scuttled backwards, his narrow backside making skittering sounds.

"Wha, wha, what are--"

Pip reached down and put a hand on the man's shoulder. He could feel Moldor's body vibrating with fear.

"There is no need for worry, Moldor," he

said. "These are friends of mine, as are the dragon warriors. They are here to help us in our quest."

With drooping eyelids, Moldor looked up at Pip.

"F-friends . . . you are being friends with . . . such as these--"

"Careful what you say, my friend," Pip said. "You do not want to offend them, especially Walu. He is very sensitive."

Moldor's head swiveled and he stared goggle-eyed at the two dragons. They were now sitting quietly, but looking around for something to eat. The succulent grasses they were accustomed to in Draconia were in short supply here in this part of Alluria.

"B-but, those are b-being d-demons. How can you--?

"That is the second time you have looked at the dragons and called them demons," Pip said, cutting him off. "Yet, you and everyone else we've talked to in Alluria deny ever having seen the demon. How can this be?"

Moldor blinked. "I am not sure; for some reason when I am seeing those beasts, I am thinking of—what are you meaning, the second time?"

"Never mind," Pip said. "It would seem that you have a memory somewhere in your mind that ties your demon with dragons. The dragons you see here are *not* demons, but valued friends of Draco and Tyco, two warriors who I trust with my life. As for the others, they are also trusted friends." He pointed at the four Folk.

"If that is what you are w-wishing, I w-will be trying."

"Good," Pip said. "Now, tell us how far it is to our destination?"

"As I am saying before, more than one day. We me must camping one night . . . is not good idea, coming to mountain in dark."

"Very well, then. We will stop and make camp before nightfall, and continue our journey at sunrise."

After they remounted, Moldor moved his horse up to ride alongside Pip, and for the rest of the ride never got more than an arm's length away. That evening, when they made camp, Moldor was like a second shadow, never more than two hand spans from Pip, and even insisted on putting his bedroll between Pip's and the fire.

As Pip lay on his blanket looking up at the inky black, starless sky, he could hear Moldor's snores, the only sound other than the crackling of the fire.

The last thing Pip heard before falling asleep was Vera's voice in his head, *I hope, cousin, that you know what you are doing. I do not trust these Allurians. Keep your eyes open.*

He could not comply with her last instruction. His eyes were tightly shut before the echo of her voice faded.

—

FOURTEEN

It was only the sky turning a lighter gray that told Pip that morning had arrived. The area through which they traveled was covered in some kind of grayish haze that blocked sight of the sun, but still enabled them to see the ever present vulture like birds soaring high above. The closer they got to the Mountain of Dark Spirits, the more oppressive the atmosphere became. Pip could understand why no one chose to live here.

The path upon which they rode became ever narrower, with huge boulders on both sides scattered along ground that rose from the path to the base of the surrounding rock walls. The boulders looked like hunched dwarves, set to pounce down upon them. The rocks, Pip thought, seemed to move. *They are moving!* He involuntarily sent his thoughts out to the others. Everyone save Norbert and Moldor came to a halt, looking around them. Norbert and Moldor, seeing that the others had stopped, pulled their horses to jerky halts as well, looking around curiously.

What is moving? Vera asked.

Valdar right, Walu said. *Something move in rocks.*

Pip sent a mental probe in the direction he'd seen movement. At first he sensed nothing, but soon he began to get the impression of many slow minds, like dying embers in a fire, so weak they barely registered.

There is someone or something there, he sent. *I can get no sense of what or how many, though.*

Vera rode up beside him. She turned to look in the same direction as he, and after seeing in which direction he probed, sent her own probe out to augment his.

Ah, she sent. *I too sense some form of being, not really an animal, but not quite human. There are many of them, and they seem to communicate with each other. Tamara, check the other side of the path. I think they have us flanked.*

Silently, the wood fairy turned her nut brown face to the opposite side of the path and probed.

Aye, Vera, she sent. *There are many there as well. They watch us, but I do not sense hostile intent.*

Moldor watched them, his brow as furrowed as theirs, only in confusion rather than concentration. He turned to Norbert.

"What do they do?" he asked.

"It would be too difficult to explain," Pip's aide said. "Let us just say they are looking out for our wellbeing."

Norbert had seen the three of them in action during the campaign against Tenkuk, and while he didn't understand the fairy magic, as he thought of it, he knew it to be extremely effective. Unlike Moldor, who was on the verge of terror so complete his bladder was on the verge of releasing its contents, he was only mildly nervous, the nervousness of any soldier about to go into battle.

"You need not worry, Moldor," Norbert continued. "Prince Valdar and the two ladies are more than capable of dealing with whatever is about; that is if the others here don't take care of it first."

"You are seeing these creatures fight before?"

"More than that, my friend; I've had the great honor to fight at their side. There are none better than these."

The two dragons, quiet until that moment, became restive, tossing their great heads from side to side and sniffing the air.

"The dragons sense something near," Draco said. "And, they do not like it, whatever it is."

"I smell something," Walu said. "Not smell good. Like bad meat too long in sun."

Nork sniffed the air. "I smell something," he said. "Not bad smell, but not good smell. Seem familiar."

"Draco, can you and Tyco fly up and see if you can see what it is?" Pip asked.

"Aye, that be a good idea, Pip," the dragon warrior said.

The two Draconians shared a look and then made clicking sounds. The dragons, belying their bulk, rose smoothly from the ground and were soon circling above the group.

Pip turned his attention from the dragons, dark shadows against the gray canopy of sky, to the darker shadows of the rocks on either side of the trail. By focusing closely, he could see furtive movements, but was unable to make out details. His mental probes only returned vague images—discordant thoughts that seemed more curious than hostile.

"Everyone gather close," he said. "I do not sense any immediate danger, but it is best to remain vigilant."

Moldor pressed his horse close to Nightshade.

"He . . . the demon, er, dragon rider, is calling you Pip," he said. "What is meaning?"

"It is a name for me, used by my friends,"

Pip responded. "It . . . has no meaning."

"You Pandarans are being very strange." Moldor shook his head. "Allurians are not having more than one name."

Pip tried not to let his annoyance with Moldor's snide remark show; if anything, it was worse than his whining. He pulled gently on Nightshade's rein to turn away. As he did so, he heard the flapping of wings signaling the return of the two Draconians.

The dragons lit gently back where they'd taken off from. Draco slid down off the neck of his beast and trotted over to Pip.

"What did you see, Draco?" Pip asked.

"Hard to tell from up so high, but there are at least thirty . . . things in the rocks, ten on the right and twenty on the left. They are small, like Nork here, and they seem to be armed with clubs. We saw no other weapons."

"Did they seem to be preparing to attack?"

"No, they seemed to just be following and watching, but I cannot be sure." He glanced at Nork. "You can never tell about trolls."

Pip bit back a smile. Not everyone had entirely come to terms with the idea of peaceful relations among all the beings of the five lands.

"Nork is not such a bad sort," he said. "His bark is far much worse than his bite . . . although, I must admit, he is quite handy with a weapon."

Draco grunted. Spinning on his heels, he

went back to his dragon. The animal lowered its neck and he mounted. Nork walked up to Pip, looking up with a malicious gleam in his eyes.

"Dragon man not like trolls, eh?"

Pip laughed. "Oh, I forgot; you trolls have sharp ears. I am sure he did not mean anything by what he said."

"Not matter. Trolls not like dragon warriors either. They not smell good."

"I do wish you trolls and Draconians would learn to get along."

"Nork willing. Up to dragon man," Nork said and walked away.

Pip turned to see Vera smiling at him.

"Okay," he said. "What is on your mind?"

"I was just thinking . . . you were anxious to get back into the field. Are you now wishing that you were back in Lands End?"

"Cousin, you read my mind."

"No, Pip, I do not read your mind," she said. "I just know how males are; always wanting what they do not have, only to realize when they get it, that they already have all they need."

Pip blinked. "I know every word you just said, but I have no idea what you mean."

"I rest my case." Vera smirked and turned away to talk to Tamara, who smiled coyly at Pip over her friend's shoulder.

Pip made a growling sound in his throat. Since learning of his heritage, he had mastered many things, foremost his ability to control the powers inherited from his father. But, try as he might, he was never able to understand the females in his life. They all spoke a language that he did not understand.

Well, he thought, I might as well concentrate on the things I *can* do well. Like, trolls with clubs skulking about in the rocks watching us.

He dismounted, drew his sword from its scabbard and faced in the direction Draco said he'd seen twenty trolls.

Raising the sword over his head, he shouted, "I know you are there. Show yourself or face the consequences."

Charles Ray

FIFTEEN

Pip felt the tension in everyone around him, squeezing him like a giant pair of clamps. The emotions he felt coming from Vera and Tamara were amazement, from the Draconians and the Folk, anticipation, and from Norbert and Moldor, sheer terror and disbelief that he would invite their stalkers to come for them.

He held his own emotions in check. It would not be good for those under his care and command to think he was not in control of the situation, even though, deep down he was not at all sure if he was doing the right thing. The problem was, he could think of nothing else to do. They had to get to the cave of the demon, not stay here and be frozen in delay by whatever lay in the rocks.

He had no doubt that he'd be able to handle the thirty trolls, assuming Draco and Tyco had counted correctly; especially with help from Vera and Tamara. He only hoped that he'd be able to do it before Norbert . . . or even Moldor . . . was injured. Too late to worry about that, he thought, as the first of the hidden enemy revealed itself.

It was indeed, as Draco had said, a troll, but the largest troll Pip had ever seen. Two hands taller than Nork, and as broad in the shoulders as Gork or Gellum, it still walked with the bowlegged, shambling gait of all trolls, and carried a three-foot long wooden club in its gnarled hands. Unlike Nork, who was a pinkish-gray and bald, this one was dull gray and covered in a gray fuzzy fur, and wearing a leather-like singlet. Behind it, Pip could see several similar looking beings peering over the rocks.

The troll walked to the edge of the rock field and stopped, placing its club on its shoulder, looking intently at Pip with its pink eyes, and a frown on its thick lips.

"Who are you, and why are you following us?" Pip asked.

"I am Tabor, and you are in land of rock trolls. Why you here, soft skinned one?"

His tone was challenging, no nonsense. Pip did not doubt that Tabor would fight if challenged, or that those hidden behind him in the rocks would as well. While Pip didn't mind fighting, his preference in this case was to pass peacefully. He had no quarrel with the rock trolls.

"We only wish to pass through," he said. "We seek a cave in the mountain, and a . . . being that lives within that cave."

"You outsider, outsider not allowed go spirit mountain."

Nork pushed up beside Pip.

"I am Nork," he said. "I am troll like you. This one," He jerked a thumb up at Pip. "He with me. We go mountain together."

"You puny, hairless cub," Tabor said, his lips curling into a sneer. "You not go mountain. You go home to mother before I smash you like worm."

Nork started forward, but Pip put a hand on his shoulder and shook his head.

"Tabor, we do not wish to fight you," Pip said. "If you will allow us to go ahead in peace, there will be no need."

The rock troll laughed; a harsh, grating sound that caused an itching sensation in Pip's ears.

"You, puny human, go where Tabor say you go; and Tabor say you turn around and go home. And, take puny . . . troll thing with you."

A loud growl echoed in Pip's ear, and he felt hot breath on the back of his neck. He turned to find both dragons behind him, with Nightshade between them.

"Pip, you want us to teach these gray monkeys some manners?" Draco asked.

His dragon stuck its long tongue out and bared its fangs.

Tabor looked nervously up at the two beasts, but he stood his ground.

"Interesting, human," he said. "You have many strange animals with you. You still go back."

Pip was impressed. Most creatures, facing a dragon, would be running away, screaming in fear. The troll was clearly afraid, but he refused to back down.

"I admire your bravery, and I do not wish to harm you, but we *will* pass here. We can do it peacefully, if you are wise, but if not, so be it."

Tabor glared at Pip through narrowed eyes, and then at the dragons. He snarled and raised his club.

"Kill them!" he yelled.

Dozens of fuzzy gray heads popped up from behind rocks in front of Pip. He heard shouting to his rear, knowing that meant more rock trolls coming from behind him. The dragons roared, Walu roared, and Moldor screamed like a little girl. Ashen faced, Norbert drew his sword and rushed to Pip's side.

"Vera, Tamara," Pip shouted. "Take the ones to the rear. I will take care of these. Do not kill them, but you may singe their fur a bit."

"With pleasure," Vera responded.

Pip took a deep breath and flung his

hands outward toward the oncoming trolls.

At first, only glittering sparks erupted from his fingers. But, those sparks soon coalesced into balls of flame the size of Pip's head, which sped away from his outstretched hands, directly toward the attackers.

Some of the trolls, their eyes bright with fear, tried to stop and turn back, while the hardier, braver, or just more foolhardy among them continued to press forward. It didn't matter. Pip's fireballs crashed among them, singing their gray fur with a sizzling sound, which was soon overpowered by their screams.

Pip closed his hands, extinguishing the flames before they had a chance to do more than turn the trolls' fur to crispy black stubs and just toast their outer skin enough to give them a taste of what could have been. Behind him, Vera had done much the same, but Tamara had added her own twist; she'd turned the ground beneath their attackers' feet to mush, causing them to sink up to mid-calf, then she'd solidified it, trapping them in place.

One troll, particularly fleet of foot, had escaped the fireballs and approached Pip from his left. Pip saw him out of the corner of his eye, but before he could send a fiery present his way, Norbert stepped up and slammed the flat of his sword across the poor unfortunate troll's nose, smashing it and sending gouts of blood and snot flying.

Screaming, the troll dropped to his knees, his hands covering his ruined snout.

The stench of singed hair was heavy in the air.

Tabor lay in a tangle of moaning, whimpering trolls. Slowly, and groaning as he did so, he pushed himself to a sitting position, and stared in awe at Pip who stood casually looking back at him.

"Have you had enough?" Pip asked.

Tabor's thick lips turned down in a snarl, only to change to a gaping 'O' of astonishment as a shadow fell over him. He looked up to see a dragon, its maw wide open, hovering just ten feet over his smoking head. Draco looked down at him, a feral grin on his ruddy face.

"Think carefully, laddie, before you answer that question," he said. "My beastie is a wee hungry, and it has been a long time since he has tasted troll meat."

Had Tabor's skin not already been pasty gray, it would have turned that color at that moment. His lips quivered and great tears formed in his eyes. A great warrior who had never been defeated before, he was wise enough to recognize defeat, especially when it stared at him from such close proximity, and had such great sharp teeth.

"Yes, had enough," he said. "Let pun-, er, human and friends pass. You be sorry, though. Dark One eat your soul."

"Who is this dark one?" Pip asked.

"Not know, never see, never want see," Tabor said. "Only know he very powerful. Maybe even more powerful than you, human."

"We shall see," Pip said. He turned to Vera. "Let us move on."

They mounted. The Draconian dragons lifted into the air, and everyone else turned toward the black mountain. Just before they started, Nork walked over and stood in front of the rock troll chief, his knobby hands on his hips. He sniffed the air, still redolent with the smell of burned fur.

"Who runt now, eh? Puny human make roast of rock troll."

He snorted at the chastened Tabor, spun on his heels, and head held high, marched away.

Charles Ray

SIXTEEN

Not long after leaving the scene of their encounter with the rock trolls, Pip and his party came to the mouth of a cave. It sat squarely across the path upon which they rode like the gaping maw of some gigantic monster. What light there was from the overcast gray sky ended just inches inside the jagged walls.

"Is not looking very inviting," Moldor said to no one in particular.

Ignoring him, Pip turned in the saddle.

"We need to get wood and make torches,"

he said.

Norbert rushed to the side of the path and soon returned holding five medium length branches in his arms.

"This is all I could find on the ground," he said. "I tried breaking some off from the trees, but it was impossible."

"This should be sufficient," Pip said. He took the branches from Norbert and gave one each to Vera, Tamara, Norbert, Walu, and Draco.

"Am I not getting one?" Moldor asked.

"You just stay close to Norbert," Pip said. "I will take the lead. Draco, you will be with me; Tyco, you and Walu will come last, and watch our back trail, just in case our rock troll friends decide to change their minds about letting us proceed."

"I will be right behind you," Vera said.

"Good, then Norbert, you and Tamara position yourselves so the entire column has light enough to see. I do not want anyone stumbling in the dark of the cave and injuring themselves."

After everyone was arranged to his satisfaction and the branches were aflame, Pip nodded at Draco and the two of them entered the cave.

The rock ceiling curved into the darkness above them, farther than the light from their torches could reach. Inside the entrance, the cave widened out, and like the ceiling, when they stood in the center, the walls were shrouded in darkness. Pip debated walking close to a wall, but decided it was probably best to stay to the center of the space. He took a deep breath and began walking forward into the unknown darkness. The path curved slightly, and shortly, they could no longer see the light gray of the cave entrance behind them. They walked in an elongated oval of flickering amber light, which cast multiple versions of their shadows to the front, rear, and sides. But, they could feel the darkness around them, pressing down like a great weight. The only sounds were the shuffle of their feet against the rock floor, the huffing of the dragons, and a faint whispering sound that seemed to come from somewhere far to their front.

They walked for what seemed like hours. In the darkness, with nothing to mark their position, and no way to mark the passage of time except counting the beats of their hearts, everyone, Pip included, felt nervous.

When the whispering became louder, now sounding more like dry leaves being blown across a forest floor, the skin at the back of his neck itched. He called a halt, and then sent a mental probe ahead into the darkness. The images and sensations he got back, like something dark and evil writhing in darkness were like nothing he'd ever experienced. For reasons that he could not fathom, he felt an overwhelming sense of dread, of impending doom.

He swallowed hard. It would not do to let the others see the fear he felt deep within his breast. He slowed his pace, thrusting the tendrils of thought deeper into the darkness. Whatever it was, it was coming closer.

The breath of Draco's dragon was hot on Pip's neck as the beast closed in behind him. Nightshade's flanks quivered and the black stallion's ears stiffened. Pip's uneased soared higher.

The torches cast a dim light about fifteen to Pip's front. When he saw the edge of that light flicker and waver, a cold gripped his chest like pincers. When the first head emerged clearly into the light, his breath froze in his throat. The dragon, now alongside Nightshade, hissed angrily, and his rider swore. Nightshade's hooved slid to a halt, sending sparks flying.

Draco leaned forward, peering over his dragon's head.

"By the shades, is that--"

"Snakes," Pip said hoarsely.

Behind him, Pip heard Moldor squeak.

"Fleeing we must," he said.

"No, we go forward," Pip said. "The dragons can deal with a few snakes."

"Aye, they can, but I think the cavern is not wide enough for both beasts to fight side by side," Draco said.

"Is doomed we are," Moldor cried.

"Not yet," Pip said. "Vera, Tamara, come and stand beside me."

He kept his eyes on the writhing mass of snakes edging into the light from the torches, but felt Vera and Tamara as they flanked him.

"We need to see what we are dealing with," Vera said.

She raised her hand, scrunched her eyes tight; and a ball of light, the size of an apple, appeared in her palm. Throwing overhand, she put the ball a few feet above and behind the snakes they could see. The ball lit up a large area, larger than that illuminated by their torches, and what it revealed sent shivers down Pip's spine.

As far as the light reached he saw snakes. Stone vipers, constrictors, asps, and many he didn't recognize, so many they crawled over and entwined with each other, all of them deadly.

"I should have thought of that," Pip said. "We could have used that instead of torches."

Vera patted his shoulder.

"You cannot think of everything, cousin," she said. "And, even we Folk are unable to hold the light orb long, so they would not have been good torches. More importantly, there are many hundreds, mayhap even thousands of snakes just yonder, and they grow nearer with each heartbeat. What will we do?"

What indeed, Pip thought. Nothing he'd faced so far had prepared him for this, and it was not just his life at stake, but the lives of the others. He could order them to turn and flee the cave. Even the dragons, unable to fly in the confines of the cavern, should be able to move faster than the snakes. He, though, had sworn to assist Princess Miko. Could he flee? His honor was at stake.

"Mayhap you should take the others and go back to the entrance, cousin," he said.

"And you, Pip, what will you do?"

In that instance, he knew what he *must* do.

"Queen Daphne sent me to help, and Princess Miko asked me to do something. I swore to both that I would."

"Then, cousin, I stand with you," she said. "Tamara, take the others and return to the cave entrance and wait for us."

"No," Pip said.

"No," Tamara said. "I stand with my sister."

"I am with you, Pip," Draco said. "And, that goes for Tyro as well."

Walu put a hairy hand on Pip's shoulder.

"Walu speak for Folk," he said. "We stay with Valdar."

"I cannot abandon my duty as long as I am your aide," Norbert said.

Moldor made a whimpering sound.

"Is crazy, all of you," he said. "Is staying here to die. Is going back we all should."

"You are free to go back to the entrance, Moldor," Pip said. "Norbert, give him your torch."

Moldor blinked rapidly. He looked at the oncoming snakes. He looked at Pip. Then, he turned and looked back into the darkness through which they'd already come. He turned back and shook his head.

"Is not liking being alone," he said. "Is staying with you."

Pip turned back. The lead snakes, a mass that stretched from one wall of the cave to the other, was not less than ten feet away and moving inexorably closer.

"I hope you have some bright idea for getting us out of this, cousin," Vera whispered. "Because, I hate snakes even more than I hate field mice."

Pip had no experience with reptiles, unless dragons counted as reptiles. They did resemble gigantic snakes with legs. In Pandara there were few snakes, and during his stay in the Land of Fire, he'd seen none. He assumed that fire would kill them, just as it would any living creature, but there were so many, he wondered if he, Vera, and Tamara would be able to create enough fire to consume them all.

As if able to read his mind, Tamara, who stood to his left, said, "There are too many of them. We will not be able to kill them all. The nine of us do not have enough weapons . . . or power I fear."

"There be *ten* of us, Lady Tamara," Norbert said with an offended tone. He unsheathed his sword and stepped up beside her.

She smiled at him. "Of course, young Norbert," she said. "Forgive me. Your sword is welcome." She punched him playfully in the arm.

Ten against thousands. Not enough, Pip thought, not enough by half. There had to be a way, though. He remembered his lessons with Hermes. The sage old man, whenever Pip despaired of solving a problem he'd posed would always say, "Ye must never think in that way, young one. Every problem has an answer, ye must but search for it. Every enemy has a weakness, ye must use it to thy advantage."

Okay, he asked himself, what weakness does a snake have? What did he know about the repellent cold blooded creatures?

Cold blooded! Yes, he thought. Snakes, unlike dragons or other creatures, were cold blooded. They reacted to the temperature of their environment, preferring moderately warm weather to colder temperatures. They, in fact, became dormant in winter. Or, so Hermes had told him when they discussed the different creatures.

"Pip," Vera said. A worried tone had crept into her voice. "They draw closer. What do we do?"

"Tamara," Pip said. "How much water can you summon up?"

The brown-skinned girl sniffed the air.

"There is much moisture in the air," she said. "As much as needed; why?"

"I have no time to explain," Pip said. "Just summon a sheet of water beneath that oncoming horde of snakes, and do it as quickly as possible." While she screwed her face up in concentration, he turned to Vera. "As soon as the water is there, you and I will freeze it."

"Wha--?" Vera started to ask, then her eyes widened and she slapped a hand to her forehead. "Of course! Excellent idea, cousin. Why did I not think of that?"

"What do you want the rest of us to do?" Draco asked.

"Just wait," Pip said. "If this works, we will be able to walk past them without harm."

The Draconian looked skeptical, but just shrugged.

The stone beneath the snakes began to shimmer. Pip noticed streamlets being pushed ahead by the serpentine movement of the horde, which was now no more than five feet away; so close, their hissing echoed off the walls around them.

"Now, Vera," he said.

He focused on the area beneath the squirming snakes, imagining the ice on the peaks of the tallest mountains. Slowly, the dark stone began to lighten and glisten. Then, the hissing decreased in volume and the writhing movement of the serpents slowed. Within seconds, the floor of the cave glistened white, and the snakes no longer moved. The hissing wound down, like air escaping through a whole in a cow's bladder, and then ceased.

Pip let his body relax, and took in a deep breath. Beside him, Vera's shoulders slumped. She too breathed hard.

"T-they are being dead?" Moldor asked.

"No," Pip said. "The cold has caused them to sleep. They will not awaken until the ice melts. By that time, we should be far from here. Let us move on."

"Uh, but, we have to walk on them," Vera said in a small voice.

"They will not feel it," Pip said. "It will do them no harm."

He did not believe in killing any creature unless absolutely necessary.

"It is not *hurting them* that concerns me," she said. "It is *touching* them, even through the bottom of my boots that concerns me. I told you, I do not like snakes."

"If it bothers you, milady," Draco said. "You can ride with me on my dragon."

Vera looked up at the smirking Draconian, and at his dragon.

"If there is anything I like less than *stepping* on snakes," she said. "It is *riding* on a giant snake. I will walk, thank you."

SEVENTEEN

They walked for more than one hundred yards before reaching the rear of the mass of snakes. Vera did not stop shivering until they'd gone around a bend in the path and could no longer see them when they looked back.

"I hope the ice has melted, and they are gone before we come back this way," she said.

Pip doubted they would be gone, and they would have to freeze them once again on the return trip, but decided that Vera, in her current mood, would not appreciate hearing that.

The cavern narrowed as they traveled, so much so that they were able to catch glimpses of both walls from the center, especially where large rocks protruded. Although it had only been a few hours since their encounter with the rock trolls near the cave entrance, it seemed to Pip that they'd been traveling for days. The sound of their footsteps on the cavern floor echoed off the walls. That and their breathing were the only sounds.

The darkness outside the perimeter of their torchlight began to seem less oppressive. Pip noticed that he could see more details of the rock walls. At first he wondered if the tunnel was getting narrower, then he noticed that he could see more and more detail, including the texture of the rock wall, and some kind of greenish mold or fungus that glowed. It was getting lighter. This was confusing. They were going deeper into the mountain. It should be getting darker.

But, sure enough, there was soon enough light from the green coating of the tunnel walls they no longer needed their torches. The way was lit as brightly as a country lane on a moonlit night. Pip had them extinguish the torches and pile them neatly against the cave wall to be available for their return journey.

His mood of depression lifted. He began to feel that he actually might be able to successfully complete his mission. There was a tinge of sadness, for he would have to slay the demon, and he was not totally convinced that this was the right thing to do. He had decided that, his promise to the princess notwithstanding, he would not immediately slay this demon. So far in the quest, no one and nothing had died—not the rock trolls, who only suffered the indignity of having their fur singed; not even the poisonous serpents, who would be able to slither away unharmed once the ice beneath them melted. If he could somehow convince the demon to no longer plague the people of Alluria, it would, in his mind, be a more successful mission than it would if he had to slay it.

As he came around another bend in the tunnel he noticed something strange. While the tunnel had curved slightly right or left before, the turns were now more numerous and more acute, some seeming to almost double back upon themselves—it was as if they were entering some kind of maze. Yet, the light from the walls did not diminish.

Then, so suddenly it caught Pip unawares, they *were* in a maze. The tunnel walls were suddenly so close they were forced to walk single file, and there were so many twists and turns that when Pip looked over his shoulder he could only see two people behind him.

"The way is too narrow for the dragon,"

Draco called from somewhere behind him. "What should we do?"

"Return to the place before it became so narrow," Pip said. "And, wait for us there."

There was a sound of scuffling and grunting as the two dragon warriors complied with Pip's instructions.

"I wonder how long they will have to wait," Vera said. She had come up close behind him.

"I hope not too long. I am sure if we are delayed too long, they will find a way to try and come after us. The Draconians are among the most adaptive warriors I know."

There was nothing more to say. Pip turned and resumed walking forward, hoping that he didn't lead them into a blind alley or some other danger. The space they were in was too constricted to allow a proper response if they were attacked. The only advantage, he hoped, was that whoever attacked them could only hit one at a time, giving those in the rear time to turn and flee—unless they were attacked from the rear. He tried to purge that thought from his mind.

Again, the time seemed to stretch on interminably. Pip could not gauge the distance they'd walked, and though it seemed like a great distance, the way the path twisted and turned, he feared they'd made little forward progress.

And then, just like that, the maze ended.

The walls, that had seemed to be closing

on him, were suddenly replaced by open space. Pip looked to his left and right. The walls now seemed miles away. He found himself in a great chamber; its domed ceiling so high above him it looked hazy. But, the light was still bright enough to see by. He looked ahead. The far wall seemed far away indeed, a wide expanse bathed in a light green glow. At the bottom center of the expanse was a dark area that looked like a small entrance.

Pip stepped aside to allow what was left of his party to exit the narrow tunnel. There were gasps of relief and surprise as they did.

They started walking toward the dark area. The ground beneath them was smooth, unlike the pebble strewn surface in the tunnel. Pip looked down. The mottled green stone under his feet was unbroken, but looked as if it had been polished by thousands of servants. He could see his blurry reflection in the surface.

Why is it different here, he asked Vera.

I do not know. Why do you not speak aloud?

I do not want to frighten the others.

Vera laughed aloud. *If the others feel the same as I do, they are already frightened. Or have you not noticed that?*

He had not. He'd been so preoccupied with his thoughts of what his next move should be he'd completely forgotten to pay attention to those around him. If Vera was frightened, he could only imagine what was going through Norbert's mind.

I guess I had not given that much thought. I assumed that Moldor was the only frightened one in our midst.

This time Vera didn't laugh, but she reached over and punched Pip's shoulder.

Are you trying to tell me that you are not scared, cousin?

Was he scared? Well, he was afraid he would make a bad decision that might get one of them hurt. He was afraid he would make a decision that was so stupid everyone would know that he was unfit to command Pandara's army. With all these fears, he had little room left to be afraid of the perils awaiting them—or, at least, he'd not really thought much about them. He was tempted to tell his cousin that he wasn't afraid, but he remembered something Valdun had said to him during one of their private conversations during his initial training period, *"When thee has responsibilities over others, thee must let them know that thee understands them. They must think thee capable, but also like them."* He hadn't understood it at the time, but later, when he fought side by side with the Folk and the soldiers of Pandara, he realized that those under his command looked to him for guidance, but they felt better knowing that he understood their fears and concerns, that when they were cold, he too was cold.

Yes, cousin, I too am afraid. But, I cannot

let the others know.

Do not worry, cousin, your secret is safe with me.

Now that she'd brought the subject up, Pip began to dwell on his worries. Should he be worried more about what lay ahead? Perhaps, but until the danger arrived, there was little he could do about it. There were, he thought, only so many ways one could die. He could think of no enemy able to withstand the powers he'd been born with, and which he was rapidly learning to master.

So distracted was he by his conversation with Vera, he'd come to the far end of the great cavern, no, more an amphitheater, before realizing it.

He found himself standing before a large stone platform, like the stage upon which Queen Daphne stood when she presided over festivals, except that hers was made of wood. Behind the stage was a large set of double doors made of some dark wood and set with brass fittings and handles. At first he thought there was no one there, until he noticed the . . . man who sat behind the desk, only visible from his sternum up. He was hairless and the color of the wood of the doors, a pair of dark brown eyes set in an otherwise featureless face. His nose was flat, a slight bump in the skin from between his eyes, spreading out into a wide triangle with two dark holes at the base. His lips were a thin line drawn straight across beneath his nose.

He was as still as a statue, looking in fact like a statue carved from the same wood as the door.

The man was so still, Pip began to suspect that he *was* a carving, but as he moved to walk around the desk to the doors, the large, bald head turned to follow his movement.

"Where do you think you are going?" The voice boomed, echoing off the walls. The lips hardly moved, but the dark eyes speared through Pip.

"Uh, pardon, sir," Pip said. "I seek a demon rumored to reside here in this cavern. I was about to pass through yon doors."

"I have not given you leave to pass. Who are you, and why do you seek the demon?"

Pip almost divulged the nature of his mission, but something held him back— mainly the arrogant tone of the man's voice.

"That is between the demon and me. Who are you that you must give *me* leave to go anywhere?"

"I am Gorgan, Keeper of the Gate, and none may pass through the Final Portal without my permission." Drawing himself up and thrusting fleshy hands against the surface of the desk, Gorgan stared down at Pip. "Now, tell me, traveler, who are you and what is your business?"

Pip squared his shoulders and stepped forward, staring Gorgan straight in the eyes.

"I am Prince Valdar of Pandara, and these-_"

Gorgan waved a pudgy hand that seemed to fade in and out against the backdrop of the doors. He'd been looking back at Pip with unblinking eyes.

"I do not need, nor do I care to know the names of your minions, Prince Valdar of Pandara," Gorgan said. "Now, what is the nature of your business with the one who resides within?"

Pip was offended by Gorgan's imperious tone, and unsettled by his unblinking stare, but he could not afford to allow such petty issues to divert him from his mission.

"My mission is only for the ears of the one who resides within," he said, using the name Gorgan had used, and in the same imperious tone. "It is not for her *minion*."

The thin lips curled upwards in the dark brown face, causing the cheeks to puff out.

"You are one with grit, young Prince Valdar. I will be gracious and ignore your lack of manners. If you wish to pass you must first pass the challenge."

Pip's hand went to his sword. If he had to fight someone or something else, so be it, he thought; he'd come too far to be turned back now.

"Very well," he said. "Bring on this challenger."

Gorgan chuckled. "You are brave, but not exceedingly smart, and you do not hear well. I did not say *challenger*, I said *challenge*. And, it is not a physical challenge, but one of the mind and wit."

Pip's hand fell away from the hilt of his sword, but he continued to look at Gorgan with his head thrown back. He smiled. As a student in Galen's school for the town's children, Pip had always been the first to solve the old councilor's problems. He was sure he could deal with whatever this brown imitation of a statue could throw at him.

"Very well," he said. "What is your challenge?"

Gorgan held up a pudgy hand, three fingers extended.

"You, Prince Valdar, must answer three riddles. If you can answer them correctly, you will be allowed to proceed."

Pip didn't want to know what would happen if he failed to answer the riddles. But, he was sure it would involve swordplay.

"Ask your riddles," he said.

Gorgan did not respond at first; he merely sat immobile and unblinking, staring off into the distance. When he finally moved, it was just his lips.

"The first riddle: brothers and sisters I have none, but this man's father is my father's son. Who is he?"

Pip laid a finger on his nose and cocked his head to the side.

Vera stepped forward. "The answer--"

Gorgan raised a hand. His voice boomed out, "Stop! Only Prince Valdar must answer the riddle. And, you have little time left in which to answer."

"How much time?" Pip asked.

"Only as much as I decide to give you," Gorgan replied. "And what I have given you for this riddle is rapidly running out."

Drat, Pip thought. This was worse than a sword fight. At least then you could see your enemy. Here, he had to deal with this overweight brown man who did not blink, and whose objective it seemed was to drive you crazy. His mind raced as he sought the answer.

Just as Gorgan raised his finger, to tell him his time was up, Pip was sure, the answer came to him. "My son," Pip blurted out as Gorgan opened his mouth to speak. "If I have no brothers or sisters, and the father of this man is the son of my father, then it must be me, and therefore, this man must be my son."

"Well done," Gorgan said. "You have answered correctly. Now, for the next riddle. Greater than the gods, more evil than a demon; the poor have much of it, while the rich need it, but, if you eat it, you will die. What is it?"

Pip's breath caught in his throat. He fought to clear his mind and settle his rapidly beating heart. The question, as asked, seemed to make no sense. He took each question in turn: greater than the gods— nothing is greater than the gods—and, there is nothing I can think of that is—of course, he thought. The answer clicked immediately. He looked at Gorgan, a smirk of satisfaction lighting up his face.

"The answer," he said. "is *nothing.* Nothing is greater than the gods, and nothing is more evil than demons. The poor have plenty of nothing, while the rich need nothing, and if you eat nothing, you will surely die of starvation."

Gorgan nodded, or at least, one of his many chins dipped toward his chest. He didn't seem to have a neck, so Pip could only discern gross movements of his large, round head through the movement of the folds of flesh that connected his jowl to his shoulders.

"You possess great intelligence for one so young," he said. "But, do not let your rashness cause you to overestimate your ability. Here is your third riddle: he who makes it has no need for it; he who buys it has no use for it; and, he who uses it can neither feel nor see it. What is it?"

Pip's emotions were settled now. Having answered the first two riddles, he approached the third with a greater sense of confidence. He closed his eyes and let Gorgan's words float before his mind's eye, analyzing the various meanings at the speed of a bolt of lightning. The answer came to him enclosed in a bright halo. He opened his eyes and smiled.

"The answer to your third riddle is a burial

shroud," he said. Gorgan returned his smile.

"Well done. You have answered the required three riddles." His smiling lips turned downward. His unblinking eyes blazed. "But, your expression is one of arrogance. For that I am invoking my prerogative as keeper to ask one final riddle. Answer it correctly, and you may proceed. Fail, however, and the consequences will be dire."

A flicker of anger flashed on Pip's face. He began to feel that it wasn't his knowledge, but his patience, that was being tested. Hermes, during the time of Pip's training, had said that in the ancient past, there had been among the Folk certain beings that were of a mischievous bent, fairies that delighted in tormenting mundanes, as humans were known. Gorgan appeared to be such a spirit. And, patience, Hermes had told him, was the only weapon that would prevail over such beings.

"As you wish, Gorgan." Pip inclined his head, but only slightly.

The mockery was not lost on the large brown man. His lips turned downward, and he made a rumbling sound somewhere deep in his chest.

"We will see how smart you are, Valdar of Pandara," he said. "This fourth riddle is a simple one, but I promise you, the answer is not simple."

"Get on with it, old man," Pip said. "I have

business with the one beyond yonder door, and do not have all day to stand here and play word games with the likes of you."

Gorgan's eyes flickered. He still didn't blink, but he did narrow his eyes as he glared at Pip. So, Pip thought, you do not like to have your games thrust back at you, do you? He let his hand rest lightly on his sword— just in case Gorgan was about more than mere word games.

The gatekeeper finally shrugged his massive shoulders and sighed.

"Very well, then; here is the final riddle: feed me and I live, but give me drink and I die. What am I?"

The answer to that one came instantly to Pip's mind, but as he opened his mouth to utter it, he froze. Was it too simple? Was there meaning behind the meaning of Gorgan's words? Was this a trick, a ruse designed to entice him into giving the first— easy—answer, and causing him to miss the more complicated underlying answer?

No, Pip thought. That is what he wants me to think. Or, more appropriately, what he wants me to over think. The riddle *was* a simple. But, the complication in the answer, Pip was almost certain, was that Gorgan wanted him to doubt it. Oh, he was a trickster all right. But, Pip was not one to fall so easily into his trap. Trust yourself, Hermes had often told him. Your first instinct is often the correct one.

"Fire," Pip blurted out. "The answer is fire. When you feed a fire, it burns brighter, but when you give it water, it goes out."

Gorgan's face was round and plump, and with his unblinking eyes it was hard to read his emotions, but Pip was sure he saw disappointment in those cold brown eyes.

"You have passed, Valdar of Pandara." Pip and his friends started to move around the desk, but Gorgan held up both hands. "Stop, I said that Valdar has passed. Therefore, only *he* may enter the chamber."

"That is not fair," Pip said. "You called them my minions. That means that what I achieve benefits them as well. I demand that they be allowed to pass with me."

Gorgan chuckled mirthlessly.

"You are in no position to demand anything, young prince," he said. "But, do not let it be said that Gorgan is not magnanimous. I will allow two to accompany you." He pointed at Vera. "You." And, then at Tamara. "And, you. The two of you may accompany, Valdar." His eyes swept the rest. "The rest of you will remain here in my company."

Pip realized that he'd probably pushed his luck as far as it would go, and besides, the three of them should be a match for any demon.

"That is agreeable," he said. He looked at Norbert. "Norbert, you are in command until we return. We should not be long."

With Vera and Tamara flanking him, he approached the two large wooden doors. They began to swing inward. Behind him, he heard Gorgan's booming voice, "Would anyone like to play a word game while we wait?"

As they passed through the doors, they swung silently shut behind them, and they found themselves in total darkness, blackness so thick Pip couldn't see his hand when he held it in front of his eyes.

What is going on? Where are we? Vera's voice had an edge of panic; the first time Pip had known her to show such fear.

Before he could answer the inky blackness began to fade, replaced by a flickering orange glow. The light blinded him at first, but as his eyes adjusted, Pip could see that they were in a chamber with walls and floor of rough stone, much cruder than the antechamber from whence they'd just come. The flickering glow came from in front of them. Soon, it clarified, and he could see that it was from a fire, a fire that seemed to be burning rocks in a great pit. Something dark moved in front of the flames, and came nearer.

As the darkness neared, its edges became sharper, and he began to see its shape more clearly, and what he saw chilled the blood in his veins.

A dragon, twice the size of those from Draconia, loomed over him. It had sharp fangs, two at the bottom and two at the top of its gaping mouth, each as large as Pip's wrist, and as long as his forearm. A forked red tongue flicked out. The dragon didn't seem affected at all by the flames as it looked down at Pip, its yellow slanted eyes unblinking.

The mouth closed, and when it opened, the dragon spoke, its words coming out in a hiss, "Welcome, Pip of Pandara," it said. "I have been waiting for you and your friends."

Pip's mouth opened, but his voice stuck in his throat. The dragon, demon, whatever it was . . . it *knew* his name. Not the name he'd given to the Allurians, but his *true* name as far as he was concerned—the name he'd used for most of his life.

Vera's elbow in his side snapped him out of his trance.

"H-how do you know my name, and what do you mean, you have been waiting for us?"

The dragon lifted its head up and stared down at Pip along the length of its snout. Its eyes seemed to twinkle.

"I know many things, prince of Pandara," it said. "I know, for instance, that you have come to kill me."

Charles Ray

EIGHTEEN

Pip stared up at the dragon, entranced by the startling revelation that his visit was expected, as was the objective.

"If you know this," he said. "Why have we been allowed to come this far? Surely, you have no wish to die?"

To Pip, a dragon's face had only one expression—fierceness—but, a look of sadness cast a shadow over this beast's face. He could hear the sadness in its voice, which was far tenderer than he would have imagined possible from such a fearsome looking being.

"No, Pip, I have no wish to die. Like any living creature, continued existence motivates me strongly. In you, though, I sense something that was missing in those who imprisoned me here—compassion. More than that, I sense also that you possess wisdom far beyond your years. Wisdom that will compel you to listen to my story, and after hearing it, you will decide whether I am to continue to live, or whether I am to die."

He was dumbfounded. Surely this wasn't the demon he'd been told was wreaking havoc on the countryside.

"I have no wish to kill you," he said. "And, I am sensing that I do not yet know the full story of Alluria. I will, therefore, listen to what you have to say."

"Then, rest yourself, Pip of Pandara, also known as Prince Valdar, heir to the thrones of Pandara and the Land of Fire. I also bid welcome to Princess Vera and her loyal friend, Tamara of the Folk. Please be seated, and I will tell you my story."

The three arranged themselves upon the floor of the chamber. The rock was warm beneath their buttocks, and seemed to yield beneath their weight. They listened in awe and wonder as the dragon began her tale— her, because it had become clear from her voice that the dragon was a female of her species.

First, you must know that this is not my true form. An evil mage from across the Great Sea came to Alluria some six months past. At first, his evil was not apparent. He came as a weary traveler from a far land, and he intrigued the court with tales of a wondrous place. Ah, before I go further with this tale, allow me to formally introduce myself.

I am Miyako, second princess of Alluria. I ruled jointly with my twin sister Miko, since the passing of our parents, King Saito and Queen Mishiko. I see you look confused, and mayhap even skeptical, but it is true. You have met Miko. I once looked like the mirror image, for we were . . . are . . . identical twins.

But, the similarity is only in physical appearance. In personality, we are opposites, as it was meant to be. Miko is the emotional one, full of energy, who rules through her feelings, while I am the rational one, who makes decisions based upon facts rather than feelings. In this manner, the affairs of Alluria were kept in balance, for we served to counterbalance each other.

It worked well until the arrival of the mage. You have probably met him. He is now advisor to my sister; Larok is his name. When he first arrived he seemed harmless, a weary traveler who delighted in entertaining the court with his tales of a land beyond the sea. But, very quickly, he began to try and drive a wedge between my sister and me—at first, he seemed to have most of his attention on me. He tried to convince me that it would be better if I pushed my sister aside and was the only ruler.

At no time, though, was I tempted. As I have said, I am ruled by logic and fact, and I know that balance is needed for successful rule. There is need for feelings, and need for rational thought. Too much of either can lead to disaster. Needless to say, his enticements failed, and he was sorely vexed at his failure.

But, in my sister, Miko, he found an easier target for his blandishments. Ruled as she is by her emotions, the pictures he created in her mind swayed her. He convinced her that as sole ruler of Alluria, she would be able to build a better life for our people.

In order to do that, however, it was required that I be removed. He tried to convince her to have me assassinated, but, she is my twin, and we have always been close. She could not bring herself to order anyone to kill me—not that any soldier of Alluria would comply with such an order. I might be a child of logic, but I am not without certain charms—or so I am told.

Failing to have me killed, Larok summoned some dark magic and had me transported to this cavern and transformed into the visage you see before you. With me gone, he has had Miko to himself, and I am sure he is working on her emotions as we speak.

Pip could not help himself. He had to ask a question, so he broke into Miyako's story.

"But, when I was there, the Princess Miko seemed to be in command," he said.

Miyako frowned at the interruption.

"Yes, Pip," she said. "It would be in Larok's interest for Miko to appear to be in charge. But, believe me, she is not. He controls her mind—oh, not completely, which is why he had her ask for help from outside the kingdom. If you will but be patient, I will explain."

Pip's cheeks flamed.

"Forgive me . . . Princess Miyako," he said. "Please, continue your story."

You are forgiven. You do make a good point. Larok's control of Miko is not complete; it can never be complete as long as I live; for the two of us share a mental connection that cannot be completely broken even though I am imprisoned here. He must have exerted all his power to get her to order you here to kill me. Once you do, he will have full control.

And that, my friend, is what he seeks. Larok came here from across the Great Sea to conquer our lands—yes, ALL our lands. He is only beginning with Alluria. Once he controls Alluria, he plans to move on the rest.

There you have my story. Now, Pip of Pandara, what do you plan to do?

Pip sat in stunned silence for several seconds. His instincts had been right—killing the demon; Princess Miyako; would have been a mistake that could also spell the end of Pandara and the other lands. Finally, he shook himself and looked up at Miyako.

"What I do *not* plan to do is kill you," he said. "Other than that, I am afraid I have no idea. It is clear that we must stop Larok. But, if he is the one who imprisoned you here, killing him might not ensure that you would return to your original form. In fact, it might leave you in this form for eternity, and that is not something I would want to do."

"Well," Miyako said. "We are both in agreement on that."

"If we could get Larok here," Vera said. "Mayhap we could convince him to remove the spell."

Miyako's dragon eyes looked quizzically at Vera.

"And, how do you propose to do that? I do not think he would just gracefully accept your invitation," she said.

Pip and Vera shared a look. He knew without her having to say what she had in mind. Larok might be a mage, but Pip doubted that he possessed the power of the Folk, or that he was even aware of it—or he would have made the Land of Fire his first target for takeover.

"My cousin and I have . . . our ways," he said. "We can get Larok here." He looked at Vera who nodded. Her face had a fiercely serious look. "And, I am sure that we can convince him to do the right thing."

Miyako looked from one to the other. Her dragon lips curled up in what Pip assumed was a smile.

"I do believe you can," she said. "Could you bring my sister as well? I think it would be useful for her to see what Larok did to me."

"Consider it done," Pip said. "We will be back shortly."

He and Vera stood, shoulders touching.

"Can you remember the layout of the castle?" he asked.

"Yes," she said. "And, I think I know exactly where Larok will be."

"Good. You get him, and I will get Princess Miko. Mayhap Tamara should go with you, in the event Larok is reluctant to accompany you."

Vera smiled. Her eyes gleamed. "I am hoping that he will resist," she said. "But, I am still happy to have my sister, Tamara's company."

Tamara stood next to Vera's other shoulder, leaning her body in so they touched.

"We will return soon," Pip said.

The three closed their eyes and disappeared in a mist that seemed to come from nowhere.

Miyako's dragon eyes widened in surprise.

"My, my," she said to the empty chamber. "I do believe friend Larok is in for quite the surprise."

Charles Ray

NINETEEN

Pip, Vera, and Tamara appeared in an abandoned corner of the castle courtyard. They looked around carefully to make sure they'd arrived unobserved. Fortunately, it was late in the evening, and the castle servants were asleep. The night guards were focused on the exterior of the castle walls, and not the courtyard, which was vacant.

"You are sure you can find Larok?" Pip asked.

Vera punched him on the shoulder.

"Stop worrying, cousin," she said. "When we were here before I just happened to notice where his chambers are. We will find him."

"Be careful. He is very dangerous."

She grabbed his shoulders and jerked him around until their faces were only inches apart.

"I told you to stop worrying," she said quietly. "Just you get Miko."

He took a deep breath.

"Yes, of course. We meet back here as soon as we have them secured."

He didn't actually worry about their ability to overpower the mage, nor did he worry about being able to take control of Miko. He was . . . just worried. So far, the only thing he'd been able to do without mishap was answer four riddles posed by a fat brown man. At that moment, he really didn't feel like an army commander. He felt more like a child, playing at being an army commander, who would be found out at any moment.

"Stop second guessing yourself, cousin," Vera said—as if reading his mind. "You have done a good job so far. You did not kill the demon . . . Miyako immediately upon meeting it . . . her. You did not because your instincts told you something about this mission as not right. You must learn to trust your instincts more. They are never wrong."

She clapped him on the shoulder, and then she and Tamara slipped into the castle.

The two women moved as silently as a gentle breeze, making not a sound as they glided over the stones. Pip followed close behind them, veering off when he reached the corridor leading to Miko's chambers.

Peering around the corner he saw no evidence of guards, assuming Miko and Larok would see no need for such inside the castle itself. Slowly, so as not to make noise, he made his way to the door to Miko's private chambers. He waited for a moment, his ear against the door. When he heard no sound from inside, he inched the door open and slipped inside.

It took a few minutes for his eyes to adjust to the darkness, but he could sense the warmth of Miko's body in the center of the oversized bed. He could hear the soft rush of air as she inhaled and exhaled. When he could see, he saw the slow rise and fall of the bed coverings and the way the cloth curved over her form. He made his way to the bed.

Gently, he sent a probe into her mind. In sleep, the darkness was still there, but not as thick or deep as when she'd been awake. It did not resist when he pushed. It felt like pushing a finger through gelatin as he moved forward. While she didn't toss and turn in her sleep, her dreams were of turmoil. He ignored them, moving deeper to that part of her brain that exercised control and slowly, gently so as not to awaken her, he wrapped his own will around hers and urged, guided her to a deeper, more gentle sleep. When he felt the turmoil retreat, he pulled the coverlet aside, momentarily stunned by the sight of her body, covered in a gossamer, skin-hugging gown that exposed all of her womanly delights. Steeling his mind against the urgings the sight brought forth, he lifted her into his arms.

Opening the door to her bedchamber, with her in his arms, was difficult, but he finally managed to work the door open with his foot just far enough to squeeze through.

He made his way slowly back to the courtyard, arriving ahead of Vera and Tamara. He placed Miko on the stones in the shadow of the wall and waited.

The wait wasn't long. Vera and Tamara came through the arched doorway with a limp body, feet dragging on the stones, held between them. When they came near, Pip saw that the body they drug belonged to Larok. He was unconscious, and there was a large bruise on his left cheek, blood dribbled from between his lips, and he had a large lump on his forehead.

They dumped him next to the sleeping Miko. Pip looked down at him, and then at them with a questioning look.

"He woke up before we could establish control," Vera said. She shrugged. "We had to resort to . . . physical measures."

"He started an incantation," Tamara said. "So, I hit him in the mouth to stop him. I am afraid I also knocked out two of his teeth."

"Of course, that didn't stop him," Vera added. "He reached for a sword, so I had to hit him . . . twice . . . before he fell unconscious."

"After that, it was easy to establish mental control," Tamara finished. "He should awaken in an hour or so. He will have a headache, and I expect he will be in a foul mood—"

"We might have to use physical measures again." Vera had an anticipatory smile on her face.

"Never mind," Pip said. "Let us get them back to the cave as quickly as possible. Can the two of you handle . . . never mind, of course you can."

Charles Ray

TWENTY

Pip, with Miko in his arms, followed by Vera and Tamara, who drug Larok unceremoniously between them, stepped out of the cloud of mist that had suddenly formed in Miyako's chamber. Still in dragon form, she sat on the rocks, the flickering flames serving as a backdrop. Her eyes lit up when they appeared.

"Pip of Pandara," she said. "You must teach me how you do that disappearing and reappearing. It is truly amazing. Ah, I see you brought my sister and her manipulator. Did they cause you any trouble?"

Ignoring her first question, Pip responded, "Larok attempted to resist," he said. "As you can see, though, we dealt with him."

The dragon head lowered, eyes regarding

189

the unconscious mage closely.

"Ah yes, I see," Miyako said. "He fought, but you vanquished him. I do hope that these wounds are painful."

"I assure you they are, and will continue to be so for some days," Vera said with a tone of satisfaction and a wicked smile on her face.

"What must we do to rectify the situation you are currently in?" Pip asked, bringing everyone back to the task at hand.

"We must somehow get Larok to break the spell he cast," Miyako said. "But, before we do that, I wish you to wake Miko so that she can see what this monster did to me."

Pip lowered Miko until her feet were just brushing the stone floor. He held her by her shoulders so that she was facing Miyako, and then gently reached into her mind and ordered her to awaken.

Her eyelids fluttered, and she shook her head, disoriented to find herself upright instead of on her bed. When her vision cleared, and she found herself looking into the eyes of a dragon, she screamed and squirmed. Pip threw his arms around her to hold her in place.

"The d-demon! Why have you brought me here?" She struggled to get away.

"There is no danger," he said, holding her tightly.

"B-but, you were supposed to kill it. Larok said the demon had to die or we would all be in danger."

"Larok lied to you," the dragon said.

Miko's body stopped moving. She stared woodenly up at the dragon.

"Y-you can speak. How can this be? How am I here?"

Her body went slack in Pip's arms. She continued to stare at the dragon, which regarded her calmly.

"Miko, do you not recognize me?" it asked.

"You . . . no, it cannot be. What? How? This must be a dream."

The dragon's head dipped down, stopping inches from Miko's face.

"Look into my eyes, Miko," it said. "Do you not recognize your own sister?"

Miko's body began to tremble.

"Miyako? How can this be? Larok said he had sent you away so that you would not be able to—"

"Larok *did* send me away, Miko. He sent me here to the prison, and then he enchanted me, trapping me in this body. His hope was that with me here, he would be able to take over Alluria through his control of you."

"I do not understand," Miko said. "He said that you would try to get rid of me so that you could rule Alluria alone; that your rule would be bad for the people. That is why he said you had to be sent away."

"Do you remember the day I was sent away?"

"N-no, I do not. It is all so unclear. I . . . one day you were no longer in the castle, and when I asked Larok, he said— " Then, she turned her head and saw Larok slumped between Vera and Tamara. "He is here. Why? What have you done to him? Is he dead?"

"No," Pip said. "He is not dead, but we have him under control so that he can do no more mischief."

"I do not understand." She twisted around and stared at Pip. "I remember; you were to kill the demon . . . now, I remember; Larok said I was to order you to kill it. But, why would he change my sister into a demon and then have me order her killed?"

The dragon's eyes looked sad.

"It was necessary in order for him to gain final control over you," it said. "Had I been killed by your order, you would have fallen completely under his sway, and through you, he would have taken over Alluria. You would have been forever enslaved to his will."

Miko collapsed. Only Pip's grip kept her from sinking to the ground.

"What have I done? Oh, Miyako, how can we change you back?"

"Now that you know his evil plans, he will no longer have control of your mind, sister. I believe our friends here will be able to convince Larok to reverse the spell he cast on me."

Vera curled her free hand into a fist.

"I will be most happy to do that," she said.

"Wake him up," Pip said.

Vera closed her eyes and wrinkled her brow. Larok groaned and stirred. His eyes opened slowly. As he took in the scene before him, and felt the tight grip of hands on his arms, he shook himself.

"What happened? Where am I?" he asked in a hoarse voice.

Pip loosened his hold on Miko. She reeled, but remained standing. He walked over and stood facing Larok.

"You are in the Mountain of Dark Spirits," he said. "In the cavern in which you imprisoned the Princess Miyako."

"How came I here?"

"We brought you here," Pip said. "You are not the only being with powers. Now, you will reverse the spell you put upon Miyako."

As his vision and senses cleared, some of the arrogance Pip had seen upon first sight of the man returned. Larok took a deep breath and attempted to jerk his arms from Vera and Tamara's grip. But, the two were too strong. He glared at them in turn.

"Ah yes, I remember," he said. "These two females accosted me, and struck me down. So, puny ones, you think you have powers? I am the greatest mage of my land. One word, and I can turn you all into insects. You dare accost me! I will show you the meaning of power. *Transmor—*"

Before he could finish the sentence, Pip raised his hand, and Larok's words died in his throat. His mouth worked franticly, but no sound came forth.

"You have the power of words, Larok," Pip said. There was menace in his voice. "But, I have the power to stop words." Pip sent an aggressive probe into the man's mind, boring past the darkness and into the deepest recesses of his brain. "I also have the power to know your innermost thoughts. I know what you wish to say as soon as you wish it." He was also able to see the vague outlines of the man's plans to first take over Alluria, to establish a foothold for his people to come from across the Great Sea to assault the rest of the lands. "You will not take over Alluria, and if your people are wise, they will come in peace, or not come at all."

Larok's eyes goggled. He could feel the white heat of Pip's probe, and was helpless against it.

"Now," Pip continued. "You will reverse your enchantment of Miyako. Do not attempt anything else. If you do, not only will I stop it, but I will stop your heart from beating."

Pip wasn't at all sure he could do that, or that he would even if he could, but Larok didn't know that. That Pip had so easily controlled his voice, and the feeling of Pip inside his mind was what he *did* know, so Pip let his imagination fill in the blanks. The man's pasty complexion became even paler.

"Do you agree to this?" Pip asked. "I grow impatient."

Unable to speak, Larok bobbed his head up and down.

Pip waved his hand. Larok made a squeaking sound. His lips quivered. The hands on his arms tightened like metal bands around a barrel.

"Do it now," Vera said. "Or I will snap the bones of your arms."

Larok swallowed hard, and took a deep breath.

"*Transmorgicum reversum,*" he said hoarsely.

There was a bright flash of light, and the dragon was enveloped in a gray cloud that sizzled and cracked. When the mist cleared, Miko's twin stood there, dressed in a white silken blouse and dark blue pantaloons. Larok opened his mouth, but Pip waved his hand, and the man's mouth gaped open, but no sound came forth.

"That will be all from you," Pip said. He turned and bowed to Miyako. "Princess Miyako, I am honored to make your acquaintance."

She inclined her head slightly. "The honor, Prince Valdar of Pandara, is all mine." Then, rushing forward, she embraced Miko, who collapsed into her arms.

"Oh, Miyako," Miko said. "Can you ever forgive me?"

"Miko, my dearest sister," Miyako said. "You are not to blame. This monster took advantage of the fact that you are ruled by your emotions. It would be illogical for me to blame you."

The two women embraced, Miko in tears, Miyako looking both sad and relieved.

"I hate to intrude upon your reunion," Pip said. "But, what are we to do with Larok?"

Miko released herself from her sister's embrace and whirled upon the cowering mage.

"For what he did, and for what he almost made me do, he should be drawn and quartered and fed to the carrion eaters," she said. Her eyes blazed.

Miyako laid a hand on her arm.

"No, sister," she said. "That would make us as evil as him. There is a more fitting punishment." She turned to Pip. "But, we will need your help."

Pip breathed a sigh of relief. While Larok *was* evil, he had been subdued, and Pip could not bring himself to kill even an enemy prisoner.

"I am at your service, Princess Miyako," he said. "What would you have me do?"

Miyako smiled. It was not a friendly smile, nor was it evil. It was a smile such as he'd seen on Vera's face when she was about to mete out punishment to an enemy—short of killing him.

"Larok imprisoned me here; I am willing to forget that he decided that exile and imprisonment was insufficient and sought to have me killed; I propose that we give him a taste of his own medicine. Can you immobilize him here in this chamber?"

"Of course," Pip said. "For how long?"

"I am tempted to say for eternity, but I think just long enough for us to depart would be sufficient."

"I can do that, but will he not escape once we are gone?"

She laughed.

"I do not think so," she said. "This place was discovered by our great-great grandfather many years ago. Once sealed into this chamber, one can only leave when the sentinel outside opens the door, and that can only be done from outside. This was the place where enemies were sent to serve their punishments for ages. We have little crime in Alluria, so it had not been used since the time of my grandfather until Larok put me here. Inside here, all alone, he can work his magic as much as he will; but it cannot escape these walls."

Pip chuckled. Larok swallowed hard, and his eyes darted from side to side.

"Indeed, that sounds like a fitting punishment," Pip said. "And, when he is never heard from again, mayhap his people will rethink their plans to invade our lands. And, if I might add to your punishment, I think I will also take away his power of speech. As a mage who works with the magic of words, to be robbed of that power is the greatest punishment of all."

"I like the way you think," Miyako said. "So be it."

Larok struggled as Vera and Tamara hoisted him up on the rock where Miyako as a dragon had perched. When they released him, Pip froze him in place before he could scramble off, leaving him the ability to move only his head. His mouth contorted; opening and closing, but with no sound coming forth.

As Pip, Vera, and Tamara gathered the two princesses and began to transport them to the outer chamber, Pip's last sight was Larok's mouth opened wide in a soundless scream.

TWENTY-ONE

Norbert rushed to Pip's side when the five of them appeared in the outer chamber.

"Sir," he said. "Is all okay? You were inside there for a long time."

Then, he noticed the two princesses.

"Uh, there are two Princess Mikos. How did they get here?"

"It is a long story, Norbert," Pip said. "I will tell you some day. For now, though, we need to get outside to Draco and Tyco and get back to Alluria."

Miyako stepped up beside Pip and looked up at the bulbous brown man sitting placidly in front of the doors to the prison chamber. A smile lit up his face as he looked down at her.

"Princess Miyako," he said. "It has been a

long time since anyone from your family has been here. It is a pleasure to see you. How may I be of service?"

"Gorgan, I have a duty for you," she said. "There is a prisoner inside the chamber."

"Yes, Your Highness, I know. The advisor Larok imprisoned a dragon here many days ago." He pointed at Pip. "The young one came to visit it, I presume to kill it. You have decided to let it live? That pleases me. Your great-great grandfather never killed his prisoners."

"No, he never did. Since you know that, why did you allow Prince Valdar to enter the chamber, if you thought he was here to kill the . . . dragon?"

"I had my instructions from Larok, Your Highness," Gorgan said. "As you know, I am required to comply with the instructions of whoever puts the prisoner in the chamber, even though I was sorely distressed when the young prince arrived. I am sorry that I have displeased you."

"You have not displeased me, Gorgan," she said. "I merely wanted to know if you still had the same instructions, and it is good to see that you have. So, here are the instructions for the prisoner who is in the chamber now, and they come from me." She turned to Miko. "And, my sister and co-ruler, Princess Miko." Miko smiled and nodded. "You are to only ever allow one person to enter the chamber, and that person is . . .

Prince Valdar of Pandara."

Pip looked at her, his mouth open in amazement.

"B-but, Your Highness, I am Pandaran," he said. "Is it appropriate for a non-Allurian to be given such a responsibility?"

Miyako smiled—that wry smile of Vera's—again. She placed a hand on Pip's shoulder.

"I know of no royal decree that prohibits me from designating anyone I should chose to be the jailer," she said. "And, this way, I know that Larok will stay in that chamber for a long, long time."

That he would, Pip thought, until the end of time if he was waiting for Pip of Pandara to release him. At the moment all Pip wanted to do was get home. He'd had about as much adventure as he could handle, and wanted to get home to his family. The very word gave him a warm feeling in his chest—his family, soon to be increased by one. He wasn't sure if he wanted a son or a daughter. It would be nice to have a son; to be able to teach him how to ride and use a sword, and if he had powers, how to use them properly. But, on the other hand, a daughter would also be nice, and he thought it would make Zohra happy.

"That he will, Your Highness," he said. "That he will."

"Now, if you would be so kind," Miyako said. "I would like very much to experience this magical way you have of traveling from one place to another."

Miko smiled impishly. "So would I," she said. "Awake this time." She looked down at the sheer gown she wore. "I do wish, though, that you would have taken the time to dress me properly for travel."

TWENTY-TWO

After passing through the maze, an easier task with both Miko and Miyako to guide them using the information passed to them by their father, they rendezvoused with Draco and Tyco. The two Draconians were pacing nervously, and greeted them effusively when they emerged from the narrow passage of the maze.

"We were beginning to worry," Draco said. "Had you been gone another hour, I think we would have entered the maze, notwithstanding its confining dimensions."

Pip felt pride at the loyalty shown by the various members of the alliance he'd formed after defeating Tenkuk. Despite their differences, and there were many, they were able to pull together for the common good when it counted.

"We are fine," Pip said, and then noticing that the two men were staring goggle eyed at the two princesses, he said, "These two ladies are Princess Miyako and Princess Miko." He was not sure which of the twins had been born first, which would establish royal protocol and rank, but he'd begun to think of Miyako as the more reliable, thus, the senior ruler of Alluria. "We rescued Princess Miyako from a chamber in which the evil mage Larok had imprisoned her."

This did nothing to answer the questions racing through their minds—one being, if one princess was imprisoned, why were two standing before them, and one in a diaphanous gown that left nothing to the imagination, and who was this Larok fellow—but, they kept silent.

Well, almost silent. There was one more question on their minds, one Tyco chose to ask. "Are we now to repeat our journey through the caves?"

"Past that nest of snakes?" Vera said. She wrapped her arms around herself and shuddered. "Is there no other way out of here?"

"Do now worry," Miyako said. "I do not know how or why, but my father said that the wards placed here to guard this place will not harm those of our blood. If my sister and I lead the way, the snakes will not harm you."

Vera looked skeptical, but the self-confident expression on Miyako's face as she and her sister stepped forward somewhat allayed her aversion to reptiles. When Pip stepped up behind the sisters, though, she made sure she was immediately behind him.

They lit their torches and entered the tunnel of the snakes. Almost immediately, they could hear the hissing and scratching, and see the leading edge of the mass of writhing snakes to their front. To Pip's amazement, Miyako and Miko did not falter or break stride. They continued to walk forward, and just before stepping into the undulating mass, it parted as if someone had swept at it with a giant broom, creating a clear path through the center, wide enough for three to walk abreast. The sisters continued forward. Pip followed, glancing from side to side at the shimmer of torchlight off the serpents as they piled to the side, still entwined and writhing.

He didn't realize he'd been holding his breath until they finally emerged from the snake tunnel and the hissing sounds began to fade, and he exhaled.

"Well," he said. "Now, we only have to pass the rock trolls."

"I doubt they will trouble us," Vera said. Now that they were past the snakes, she was her normal self. "They have no more fur left to singe."

Miyako chuckled, and turned to Pip.

"And, I assume that this was your doing? You have the power to control fire?"

Pip pointed at Vera and Tamara in turn. "The three of us do," he said. "Others of the Folk have different . . . talents."

"I thought you were Pandaran," Miko said.

"I am both. My mother was Pandaran, but my father was of the Folk."

"So, the legends are true," Miyako said. "Relationships among the different people of the land are possible."

"I have heard that once upon a time, all the people lived together in harmony," Pip said.

Miko looked wistful.

"If only such were possible again," she said.

The more practical, Miyako laid a hand on her sister's shoulder.

"With an ally such as Prince Valdar and his friends," she said. "It just might be possible." She glanced at Pip. "We must discuss it when we are back in the castle."

The passage of time didn't seem as long coming out as it had going in, perhaps because they were not faced with peril at every turn, for almost before they knew it they were emerging from the entrance of the cave and onto the path where they'd encountered the rock trolls. The trolls were where they'd left them, behind and upon the rocks, fierce scowls upon their gray faces.

Their fur still hadn't grown back in, and the odor of burned hair still hung in the air.

Pip tensed as soon as he saw them, but beyond scowling, they made no move. He assumed it was the presence of the two princesses, nevertheless, he kept his hand on the hilt of his sword and his attention focused on the trolls until they went around a bend in the path and they were lost from sight.

At the base of the hill leading up to the cave, Pip called for a halt.

"Now, we must arrange getting the princesses back safely to their homes," he said.

"We could fly them there," Draco offered.

Miyako held her hands up. A frown creased her otherwise beautiful face.

"Thank you, kind sir," she said. "But, after so many days trapped in the body of a dragon, I do not think I am quite ready to sit upon the back of one. Besides, I am anxious to experience Prince Valdar . . . Pip's form of travel."

"Are you sure you can handle them both?" Vera asked.

"I do not think it will be a problem," Pip said. "I will take the two princesses. Norbert, please see to Nightshade. We will await your arrival."

Vera looked at him intently. She opened her mouth, hesitated, and then closed it.

"Very well," she said. "We will see you at

the castle."

Pip took Miyako's hand in his left and Miko's in his right.

"Are we ready, ladies?" Pip asked.

Miyako looked excited, but Miko looked skittish.

"Is it safe?" she asked.

"Oh, sister," Miyako said. "You have already done it once."

"Yes, but I was asleep, so I have no idea what happened."

"I assure you both," Pip said. "You will be as safe as a babe in its mother's arms."

Miko didn't look reassured, but she finally nodded.

"Very well, if you say so."

"Yes," Miyako said. "Let us get this trip started."

TWENTY-THREE

Pip was enveloped in the familiar grayness. He could feel the princesses' hands in his own, and he heard the squeals from both as the haze surrounded them—Miyako's one of excitement, Miko's of fear. In a few heartbeats the haze disappeared, and they found themselves standing in the corridor outside Miko's bedchamber as Pip had envisioned. He'd considered arriving in the courtyard, but since it was early morning, and servants and guards would be about, he didn't want to startle anyone. And, he thought wryly, Princess Miko wasn't exactly dressed appropriately for a public appearance. He'd also thought about making the arrival point the *inside* of her chamber, but considered that probably inappropriate as well. The corridor outside was an acceptable compromise.

As Pip released his hold on their hands, Miyako brushed at her clothing, while Miko staggered slightly, her eyes round with wonder.

"T-that was amazing," she said.

"I could become accustomed to traveling like that," Miyako said.

Pip looked around to make sure they were alone in the corridor.

"The others will not arrive until tomorrow," he said. "I do not know about the two of you, but it has been many hours since I last slept, and I am about to fall asleep standing here. I would suggest that you both get some rest. Oh, and is there somewhere where I might close my eyes for a few moments."

Miyako pointed to the door across the corridor from Miko's.

"That is my bedchamber, but since you are married, I do not suppose you would want to share it with me." When Pip's face darkened, she laughed. "I was jesting, Pip. I think that you would be comfortable in Larok's chamber, since he will not be returning. It is down this corridor, across two corridors and on the left. You should have no trouble finding it, and you should not be disturbed."

"Miyako," Miko said. "Could you join me in my chamber for a few moments before you sleep? I . . . I do not want to be alone just yet."

Miyako pulled her sister into her arms, rubbing her back.

"Of course I will, Miko," she said. "I will stay as long as you require." As they opened the door, she turned back to Pip. "Go and sleep well, Pip of Pandara. We will notify you as soon as your people arrive."

Pip waited until the door was closed before turning and following her directions to Larok's private bedchamber. He paused at each intersection to ensure the way was clear before proceeding, arriving before the plain wooden door after only a few minutes. It was unlocked. He surmised that Larok's arrogance and belief that he had power over the occupants of the castle left him feeling no need to secure his chamber. He pushed the door open and entered.

The room was as large as Miko's, but instead of wall hangings, precious metals and jewels, it was as plain as an army tent. A large bed with a plain brown coverlet sat in the far corner; a square wooden table with one straight back chair sat in the center. Upon the table lay a large book, an inkstand and quill, and a stack of papers. To the right was a bookcase filled with leather-bound volumes, and to the left on an otherwise bare wall was a large sheet of paper, which, upon closer examination, Pip discovered was a hand-drawn map of Alluria, Barbaria, and the other lands.

The map was similar to one Pip had in his own office, except, where Pip's had labeled the land south of Barbaria as 'UNKOWN,' on this map, it was labeled 'ALLURIA.' The land to the east of Alluria was labeled 'UNKNOWN,' which indicated that Larok's knowledge of the lands on this side of the Great Sea was not complete. The Great Sea occupied the entire right side and top of the map, leaving no clue to the location of Larok's homeland, or its name. While he'd been inside the man's mind, Pip had been so occupied with blocking his incantations, he'd been unable to extract any information as to his origins; he hadn't even been able to determine what Larok's people called themselves. This map, though, seemed to validate Miyako's claim that Larok had designs upon the lands on this side of the Great Sea.

Turning away from the map, Pip walked to the table. He lifted the stack of papers and examined a few; mostly administrative matters of Alluria and reports from subordinate officials in the castle. Nothing of importance. He replaced the papers and was about to turn away, when he noticed the corner of a single sheet of foolscap sticking out from under the book. He picked up the book and opened it, rifling through the pages. It was a ledger, listing the accounts of the castle; again, nothing of importance. He then lay the book down and picked up the single paper.

It was written in a precise, clerical hand, and what it contained froze the blood in his veins:

Your Most Celestial Majesty,

Your humble and obedient servant sends greetings, and begs forgiveness for the long period during which I have not communicated. The journey across the Great Sea was long and perilous, but after many weeks, I finally arrived upon the shores of the land which our seers foretold. I have now but to discover a method of sending this dispatch to you, and you can send the army to help me finish our plans to expand your great kingdom over all that lives upon all the lands and seas.

I was able to destroy my craft before being discovered by the locals, a people who call themselves Allurians. This small kingdom, I discovered, is ruled by two princesses who are only recently entered into womanhood. It was an easy matter to take control of one—the one ruled by her emotions. The more rational one was able to resist my blandishments, but I managed to wrest control of her sister, completing phase one of my plan to obtain control of the kingdom.

Phase two, which I have recently set into motion, will enable me to complete the takeover of Alluria, hopefully well before the army arrives.

The land adjacent to this, called Barbaria, will be even easier to subdue. Once ruled by an iron-fisted tyrant, and possessing a mighty army, it is now under the control of a council of landed men, the Council of Lords. The once mighty army has been disbanded, and replaced by a constabulary whose sole duty is collecting taxes and protecting the peasants from bandits that still roam the countryside.

It is the lands beyond Barbaria that will pose the greatest challenge. Pandara, the kingdom that defeated the Barbarian tyrant, is ruled by a benevolent queen, and is reported to have an army led by a young man with great powers. I doubt that his powers are greater than mine, but with an army behind him, he promises to be formidable. Thus, I will require our own army at my side when we move upon them.

There are rumors of other lands, smaller and weaker, but occupied by people who also possess magical powers. Whether this be true or not, I have yet to learn. I do believe, Your Celestial Majesty, that these lands pose an insignificant threat, and they will fall easily beneath the boots of our soldiers.

I must now focus my energy upon completion of the current phase of the takeover of Alluria. Once the stranger has slain the co-ruler, I will have full and total control of

The letter ended there, as if the writer had been interrupted, and never got the opportunity to return to it. Pip wondered if Larok had been writing this letter when Vera and Tamara arrived to convey him to the cavern. It still did not identify Larok's people or his land, but it was final proof of his dastardly plans. Pip could easily imagine that the killing of Miyako was the 'phase two' to which Larok referred.

As disturbing as the information was, it was reassuring to know that the man hadn't been in regular contact with his land or his king. Only slightly reassuring, though. When these alien invaders from across the Great Sea heard nothing from their agent, would they send another, or would they send an army to look for him? Somehow, Pip doubted the latter. If they'd been so disposed, they would have sent the army in the first instance. For whatever reason, they needed to send a spy and provocateur first. But, that plan had failed. They might be frightened and dissuaded, or they might send another. Pip would have to warn Miyako and Miko to be ever vigilant to the presence of strangers, especially anyone coming from the direction of the coast.

Now, more than ever before, he wanted to return home. Not only to be near his beloved Zohra, but he needed to warn Queen Daphne of this new danger, and prepare the army. In addition, he needed to send warning to the other lands. Their hard won unity, still in its infancy, was already under threat.

As Pip folded the paper and tucked it into his tunic, he yawned. He'd been awake for more than a day. His stomach growled, reminding him that he hadn't eaten in the same amount of time. For now, though, sleep was his first priority.

He walked to the bed. Larok's stale, musty odor still clung to the bedding, but Pip was so tired, he would have welcomed the smell of horse dung in stable straw at that point. Kicking off his boots, he fell across the bed, and lying atop the coverlet, he fell almost immediately into a deep sleep.

TWENTY-FOUR

Pip slept through the afternoon and the night, awakened by the crowing of a cock the next morning. He rolled over and sat up. After retrieving his boots, one of which he'd kicked under the bed, he put them on and stood, stretching. His muscles felt stiff and achy, and his stomach sounded like an angry wolf.

After relieving himself and washing away the dust of travel, he'd have to find some food. Fortunately for the first two, Larok had a private bath attached to his chamber. Pip could do nothing for his travel-wrinkled clothes, but his body felt much better—at least on the outside—once he'd scrubbed and rinsed away the grime from his skin and hair.

As he opened the door to the chamber and stepped into the corridor, he was met by the twins, dressed now in less revealing attire— one-piece chemises that reached almost to the stone floor and at the top only displayed a tiny bit of shoulder and area of skin above their breasts.

"Pip, you've finally returned to the land of the living," Miyako said. "It is nearing mid-day. You slept for almost one full cycle of the sun."

It took him a few seconds to realize that she was saying he'd slept an entire day.

"Yes, I guess I was more exhausted than I thought," he said. "Now, though, I am so hungry, if I do not find sustenance I will be forced to eat my boots."

The two women laughed.

"We cannot have you walking around the castle barefoot," Miyako said.

"Yes, that would be as bad as me in that cave in my . . . you know," Miko said.

Miyako poked her sister's shoulder with a slim finger.

"Oh, you looked nice; didn't she Pip?" she said.

At that moment, Pip's stomach emitted a loud rumbling growl. His cheeks flamed, and the princesses laughed so hard tears flowed across their cheeks.

"I think our guest needs food," Miko, the

first to recover, said.

"Of course," Miyako said. "Please, come with us. The cook will prepare you something. Oh, your friends have arrived, and they will meet us in the dining chamber."

The thought that everyone was back safely pleased Pip, but the thought of getting something to eat made him smile broadly.

"Lead on, ladies," he said.

The dining chamber, which was a slightly smaller version of the great hall, and located nearby, was abuzz with activity when they arrived. Norbert, Vera, Tamara, Draco, Tyco, Walu, Gork, Gellum, and Nork sat at a large square table near the entrance. Enough food to feed a small army was piled in the middle of the table, and everyone was going at it with a fervor similar to the way Pip had seen them fight. At the aromas wafting from the table, his stomach growled and contorted. He had to restrain himself to keep from rushing over.

Heads lifted, and greetings were uttered around mouths full of food. Vera pointed at three empty chairs near her. Pip and the twins sat. Norbert pushed a full plate of food in front of him. Draco and Tyco bumped into each other trying to push plates in front of the twins. It was impossible to discern which Draconian was aiming at which princess, but both women seemed intrigued by the attentions—even the practical minded Miyako. As soon as Pip fasted the first bite of a piece of meat from his plate, he ignored everything else happening at the table, and said not a word until his stomach felt it couldn't take another morsel.

Sated, he sat back and rubbed his stomach.

"Better now, cousin?" Vera asked.

"Much. I cannot believe, though, I slept an entire day."

Vera shrugged.

"You used your powers a lot; that takes a lot of energy. Look at what you ate."

Pip looked down at his plate, which looked as if it had been washed.

"That was your body's way of telling you that you needed to replenish your energy. I think you are okay now."

"I do feel better," he said. "Now, that we have all eaten, there are things we need to discuss."

Everyone pushed their plates aside, including the twins, and all eyes were on Pip. He began by explaining the letter he'd found in Larok's chambers, and how the mage had manipulated Miko in an effort to make her responsible for the murder of her sister so that his people could invade and take over Alluria, and subsequently, the rest of the lands.

"Who are these people?" Draco asked.

Shaking his head, Pip said, "I was not able to get that information from Larok. I was a bit preoccupied with trying to prevent him from enchanting me. And, I did not know of his plans until I returned here yesterday."

"Well, what are we to do?" Miyako asked.

"I think for now we are safe," Pip said. He patted her hand. "Larok had no opportunity to communicate with his people if his letter is to be believed. I think that when they do not hear from him they will hesitate to follow—or they might send another agent like him. Here in Alluria you must be vigilant regarding any strangers, especially any who come from the direction of the sea."

"You can be assured we will do that," Miyako said. "There will be no more Larok's in Alluria."

"He has already been responsible for the loss of soldiers," Miko said. "That will weigh heavily on me, for I am the one who allowed him to—"

"No," Miyako interrupted her. "I spoke with the captain of the guards this morning before you woke. Larok had several soldiers reassigned to isolated posts in the far west of the land. He then told you that they had gone to kill the demon and had been killed by it as a means to convince you to have me killed. He threatened the captain with death if he ever told. When he saw me, he knew that Larok was no longer a threat, so he confessed everything."

Miko sighed and smiled. A single tear from her left eye flowed slowly over her cheek.

"Very well, then," Pip said. "Your Highnesses, with your permission, I would like to take this letter with me. I will need to show it to my queen, and it will be helpful in convincing the other lands of the potential danger and the need for vigilance."

"And the need for us all to work together," Miyako said.

"That too," Pip said.

TWENTY-FIVE

Early the following morning, Pip and his entourage bid farewell to the twins and set out for their homes. After crossing the border into Barbaria, the Draconians and the Folk split off to go to their respective homes, with the promise to spread the word about the unknown aliens from across the sea. Pip, Vera, Tamara, and Norbert set their sights on the road to Pandara.

Pip stopped in Gondwona and held a brief parley with the Council of Lords, briefing them on the events that had transpired in neighboring Alluria. The council promised to be vigilant and swore to make forces available to aid their neighbors should these strangers invade.

Three days after leaving Alluria, they rode into the outskirts of Lands End. Pip felt pounds lighter when the chimneys and rooftops came into view.

He'd forgotten how much he liked riding along Lands End's cobblestone streets, watching merchants and artisans at work in their shops, housewives doing laundry behind neat fences, and children playing in the dirt or on grassy verges between buildings. His eyes felt warm as he passed the old tannery where his Uncle Auric, now clothier for the royal castle, once worked hour after hour tanning hides and working skins into cloth, and his Aunt Ludmilla baked some of the most delicious cakes and cookies in all of Pandara. Since moving into the castle, Auric had sold the house and workshop to a man named Krull, who had a cheerful wife, Ezmelda, who was nearly as broad of girth as Ludmilla, and who also loved to bake. Pip could smell the aroma of her bread as they passed.

They rode into the main courtyard, halted and dismounted. Norbert took Nightshade's reins and left for the stables. Vera and Tamara started to follow.

"Will you two not be with me when I inform the queen of our adventure?" Pip asked.

"I think you can handle it, cousin . . . er, commander," Vera said. "I must check with the regimental commanders to ensure my new training schedule has been implemented."

"And, I must check the warehouses," Tamara said. "I am sure they are in total disarray since my absence."

They saluted him and rushed after Norbert. He understood. As much as he loved his aunt, having to stand before her and conduct a briefing was intimidating. He'd much rather be facing an armed enemy than stand before an audience, even an audience of one, and speak.

He was anxious to be with Zohra, but knew that his duty lay in first reporting to the queen. Zohra would understand.

The guards at the entrance saluted smartly as he passed, a gesture that he absentmindedly acknowledged as he made his way to Daphne's audience chamber, a utilitarian space behind the throne room where she conducted the royal business.

When Pip arrived, she was already waiting—the castle grapevine working efficiently as usual—behind the modest wooden desk she preferred to sitting on the throne. Galen, dressed in his councilor's robes, and with a sober expression on his narrow face, sat to her left. They both eyed Pip expectantly as he walked into the room.

He bowed, first to Daphne, and then a slight inclination of the head toward Galen.

"Well met, Prince Valdar," Daphne said,

but a twinkle in her eyes and the twitching of the ends of her mouth belied her formal tone. "How was your journey to Alluria?"

Pip noticed that Galen was now leaned forward in his chair, his eyes also twinkling.

Taking Larok's unfinished letter from his tunic, Pip began his story. As he came to the part where he'd discovered the letter in Larok's chambers, he handed it to Daphne. "As you can see, Your Majesty," he said. "The letter is not finished, so I believe it safe to assume that Larok's people, whoever and wherever they are, are unaware of his fate, and therefore are likely to be reluctant to launch an invasion."

Daphne read the letter, her light brown eyes wide with shock. When she finished reading she passed the letter to Galen.

"You might be correct, Pip," she said; all pretense at formality gone now. "But, we must still be prepared. Galen, have you ever heard of lands or people beyond the Great Sea?"

The elderly councilor rubbed at the gray stubble on his chin as he read the letter.

"No, Your Majesty, I have not," he said. "But, I have not studied the ancient history of our people as closely as mayhap I should have. It does, however, not surprise me. The tales I have read talk of a time when beings of all kinds roamed the land, and before the coming of darkness and warfare, all lived together in harmony."

"It would appear that those who found themselves on the other shores of the Great Sea developed in a different direction, more along the lines that our neighbor, Barbaria, once followed."

"True," Pip said. "But, if this Larok was an example, unlike the Barbarians, these . . . people have magical powers to aid their aggression. It will take the combined efforts of everyone in the land to stand against them."

Daphne laid a finger against her carmine lips, her forehead wrinkled in thought.

"Aye, that it will," she said. "We must waste no time. I will call an assembly of representatives of all the lands to meet here in Lands End to discuss our next steps."

Galen handed the letter back to her.

"I will send messengers immediately, Your Majesty," he said.

Pip beamed with pride. His aunt, though young and beautiful, was intelligent and decisive, and as she'd proven when she'd been taken hostage by Tenkuk the Barbarian, brave as well. She was the perfect one to pull all the people together, and he would proudly stand at her right hand.

"What would you have me do . . . Aunt Daphne?"

Daphne beamed at her nephew.

"Right at this very moment, Pip, I would have you seek out that beautiful wife of yours and be at her side. I sense that her time is near."

He'd been so focused on alerting Daphne and Galen to the danger posed by some unknown enemy, he'd almost forgotten his real reason for wanting to be back home.

"Yes, please forgive me," he said. "I must go immediately to her."

Daphne and Galen were laughing as he backed clumsily out of the room. Once outside, he turned and ran through the corridors of the castle, bumping into servants too slow to get out of his way, and mumbling apologies, but never stopping until he was in the corridor at the end of which was the door to the bedchamber he shared with Zohra. He saw his foster father, Auric, pacing back and forth in front of the door, a worried frown on his fleshy face, and came to a stumbling halt just before barreling into him.

"Uncle Auric," he said. "It is good seeing you. I have much to tell you about my trip, but now I must see Zohra." The words came tumbling out of his mouth as he reached for the door handle.

Auric put fleshy hands on his chest, holding him back.

"Whoa, boy, you cannot go in there now," Auric said. "Milla and the midwife are with her. No men allowed."

"Wha-, but, I have traveled a long time, and have missed-, what do you mean, no men allowed?"

Auric raised his hands, palms up, and

rolled his eyes skyward. "Pip, only a woman understands other women," he said. "I have found it best not to question them; just follow their orders, and try to stay out of the way."

"B-but, I must see her. She might need me."

"The baby is coming, son," Auric said. His voice was gentle, as was the hand he placed on Pip's shoulder. "You would only be in the way. Trust your Aunt Ludmilla and the midwife to know what to do. For now, all you can do is join me in doing what expectant fathers have done since the beginning of time; pace back and forth here until we are summoned."

Pacing the corridor was for Pip the same as doing *nothing*, and doing nothing was not a part of his nature. But, his foster father had never told him wrong, and had always seemed to know the wise and proper thing to do. He took a deep breath. It would, he thought, be like waiting to go into battle. Until the fighting started, there was nothing to do but wait with butterflies in your stomach and gruesome images of what could be about to happen running through your mind. Maybe pacing would help control the thoughts at least.

He fell into step beside his uncle, and the two of them paced.

The time before a battle can stretch out until an hour seems like an eternity. The time Pip spent pacing the corridor a few feet from a door beyond which waited his wife made waiting before a battle seem as swift as the desert hawk diving on its prey. For a long time, the only sound in the corridor was the scuffing of his and Auric's boots as they paced, ten steps in one direction, turn and ten steps back.

Then, there was a scream, muffled by the thickness of the wooden door, but still loud enough to make the hairs on the back of Pip's neck stand on end. He moved toward the door, but Auric caught his forearm, holding him back.

"That, my boy, is another reason it is best we wait here," he said. "Giving birth is a wondrous experience, or so the women I know tell me, but it is not without pain."

He hadn't thought of that. In his thirteenth year, Auric had explained to him the difference between men and women, but no one had ever talked to him about childbirth. And, try as he might, he could not picture the process in his mind. With all his powers, he was, like all the fathers-to-be before him, helpless—helpless and useless.

"Do not fret, Pip, it is the natural way of things. Women are stronger than men. This I learned as a young man, and even though Milla and I have never had the pleasure of having a natural child, I have seen many children come into this world. It is always with pain, but afterwards, the glow I have seen on the new mothers' faces makes me know that they are strong, and they are happy for what they have endured."

"If you say so, Uncle Auric," Pip said. His shoulders sagged in defeat. "I guess there is nothing I can do but wait."

Auric smiled and patted Pip's shoulder.

"Now, you have learned the first lesson in being a good husband. Before you know it, you will be a fine father as well."

Pip smiled weakly and put his back to the wall, sliding down until he was sitting on the floor, his legs stretched out in front of him.

"Will it be like this for each child?" he asked.

Auric, a bit slower, eased down beside him.

"I do not know, son. I am told by those men who have more than one child that it does get easier with each one . . . are you already planning for another."

Pip shook his head vigorously.

"No, I definitely am not! I trust you, but I cannot take the chance that it will be this way each time. I do not think I could endure this again."

They sat in companionable silence. There were no more screams, which in one way was more nerve wracking for Pip than hearing the screams had been. That, Auric could explain; but when the silence went on for a long time, even Auric began to look nervous and uncertain.

Just as Pip could stand it no longer and

was about to ask Auric what was going on, or ignore him and barge into the chamber, the door silently swung open. Ludmilla stood there, a broad smile on her sweat-stained face. She looked down at them and heaved a great sigh.

"Just like men," she said. "We women are doing all the work and you have your lazy carcasses sprawled out on the floor."

Pip and Auric scrambled to stand.

"We were just resting," Auric said.

"How is Zohra?" Pip asked.

Ludmilla smiled and patted his cheek.

"She is fine Pip, and she is asking for you."

She stepped back into the chamber, leaving the door open. Slowly, Pip entered with Auric following behind, peering over his shoulder.

The midwife, a portly woman Pip recognized as one of the castle cooks, was bending over the bed, placing a small bundle against Zohra's shoulder. Zohra, a tired look on her face, looked down and smiled—her face brightened as she did so. When the woman moved away, Zohra saw Pip. Her smile broadened.

"Pip, you are home," she said. "You have come just in time. Come and take a look at your children."

He'd covered half the distance to the bed when her words, and what he was seeing, registered on his brain.

"Children . . . d-did you say children?"

She looked down at the bundle at her right shoulder, and then at the one on her left. *Two* bundles! How could that be, his mind screamed. He stumbled the rest of the way to the bed and knelt beside it, reaching for her hand. His head moved from side to side, taking in her flushed but happy looking face, and each of the tiny bundles in turn, and feeling as if he would faint.

"Yes, husband," she said. "We have two children; a boy and a girl. What do you have to say about that?"

"B-but, how? Did you know it would be . . . twins?"

Zohra shook her head and squeezed his hand.

"Not until just before it was time," she said. "Then, I distinctly felt two sets of feet kicking me. Are you not happy?"

"I . . . I am overjoyed, I am just surprised. I have only ever met one other set of twins, and they . . . oh, I will tell you of them later when you have rested."

Ludmilla came up behind him and laid hands on his shoulders.

"It happens sometimes, Pip," she said. "Zohra said that among her people, there are often twins, and it is considered a good sign, especially when you have one of each. What will you name them?"

Zohra carefully folded the blankets back, allowing Pip the first sight of his son and daughter. The boy, on Zohra's right arm, had thin red hair and reddish complexion like Pip, the girl on her left, had more hair, and it was as dark as Zohra's. Both had dark brown eyes which looked up at Pip as if they already recognized him, even though they were only minutes old.

"Yes, Pip, what shall we name them?" she asked.

"Uh, it is the custom of the Folk to give a name that is from both mother and father," he said. "I had been thinking that if our child was a boy, we would name him Valzo, which is the combination of our two names, and if it was a girl, to name her Dara. Now that we have both, I suppose that should be their names . . . that is, if you approve."

She smiled and patted his hand.

"Those names fit them," she said. "Valzo and Dara say hello to your father, Valdar, but we just call him Pip. Of course, you will call him papa."

The two babies pursed their mouths. Pip would have sworn they smiled. He felt a swelling in his chest and a stinging in his eyes. Leaning over, he gently kissed each of them forehead, and then finally, kissed Zohra on the lips.

"They are perfect," he said. "Just like their mother."

Ludmilla touched his arm.

"Okay, father," she said. "Time to let mother and babies get some rest after the babies are fed."

"What do they eat?" Pip asked.

Auric, who had been standing at the foot of the bed beaming down at them, laughed.

"Come on, Pip," he said. "I will explain it to you, but believe me, you do not want to be here to see it."

With a confused look on his face, Pip allowed himself to be led away.

Charles Ray

TWENTY-SIX

It was two days before Ludmilla decreed that Zohra had rested enough to withstand a visit from Pip. During this time he'd slept in his office.

When he entered, Zohra was sitting in bed, her back against the headboard. The children slept peacefully in a smaller bed that had been arranged next to the main bed.

"You are looking well," he said.

She patted the coverlet.

"Come and sit down, Pip," she said. "Yes, I am feeling fine. I am sorry you were forced to sleep in your office . . . Ludmilla told me. Did you sleep well?"

"Not really. I worried about you." He looked over at the sleeping babies. "Did you and the children sleep well?"

"Yes, they are angels. They only wake once during the night to be fed, and they seldom cry. Once I have fed them, they go right back to sleep."

They chatted back and forth for nearly an hour about the babies, and happenings in the castle during Pip's absence; everything but the trip itself.

"Now," Zohra said. "You must tell me all about your great adventure. Was it all that you hoped it would be?"

All and more, Pip thought. He then told her everything, leaving out nothing, including Miko's attempt to seduce him, which earned him a mock frown and a punch in the arm. He then told her that once the journey was underway, all he really wanted to was return home. When he'd finished his story, she laid her head against his shoulder.

"So, these two princesses, Miyako and Miko, were beautiful?" she asked.

"Yes, I suppose you could say they were pleasant to look upon."

She pinched his arm.

"And, you were not attracted to even one of them?"

"Ow, of course not," he said. "They were pleasant to look upon, but each of them was only half a woman."

She pulled away, turned and frowned up at him.

"I know that I became large while I carried our children, but I will have you know that I am *not* fat. No Avian woman is ever fat."

Pip smiled. "You mistake my meaning, dearest wife," he said. "I was not referring to their size when I said each was half a woman." He explained their diametrically opposed personalities, and how it took the two of them acting in concert to make decisions for Alluria. "So, you see, they did not have your spirit. And, for your information, I do not think of you as fat; not even when you were big with child."

She smiled. She had a mischievous glint in her eyes. Reaching up, she pulled his head down and kissed him on the point of his chin.

"So, I am the only woman for you?"

"Always and forever," he said.

"So, was your adventure all that you hoped?"

He pulled her close, burying his nose in her hair and enjoying the warmth of her body against his.

"I found that what I really wanted was right under my nose all the time," he said. "I was concerned that I might not be a good father . . . I still am . . . but, after talking to Auric, I now know that I am no different than any other man. I will learn; with your help, I *will* be a good father. As for adventure; I will go where I am needed, when I am needed, but I have no need to look for any adventure any further than the three of you. I think those two will be as much adventure as I can handle for a while."

"Then, we will have adventures together," she said, burrowing her face against his chest.

Things felt right. He was where he was supposed to be. His mind was at rest—or, almost at rest. There was someone out there, somewhere, who would do them harm. He'd been angered when he first read Larok's partial letter, but now that small part of his mind that he reserved for small matters seethed. Now, it was not just a threat to his land and his people, it was a threat to his family.

He didn't know how, he didn't know when, but he would someday, somehow find the aliens from across the Great Sea. He would try to make peace with them, but if they didn't want peace, he would teach them the meaning of war.

Author's Note

I'm not normally a fan of stories with unresolved issues at the end; I put cliffhangers at the end of chapters, but try to wrap everything up by the end of the book. Readers will note, though, that I left one hell of a big mystery unsolved in this book. Who are the mysterious aliens from across the Great Sea, and will they send someone else to prepare Pandara and the other kingdoms for invasion?

That is a question for a fourth book in the Pip of Pandara Chronicle series. That's right, at some point in the future, there will be another adventure with Pip, Vera, and the others—I might even throw Pip's children into the mix for variety, I haven't decided yet. Originally, this was to be a three-book series, but as I was working my way through this one, the idea for a fourth book kept nagging away at me, so I went back and added the invasion from abroad teaser, and deliberately left it vague, not to tease readers, but to give Pip a reason to go on another adventure.

So far, this series has been moderately well received. It's not breaking any records, but the feedback I get is mostly positive. As an indie author, feedback and reviews are almost as important as sales—naturally, sales are the greatest thing that can happen—because they tell a writer what people like, or don't like, about his or her writing. So, if you liked this book, it would be great if you could take a few minutes to leave a short review on Amazon, Goodreads, or your blog if you have one.

You can keep track of what I'm reading, and occasionally snippets from works in progress, by reading my blog, Charles Ray's Ramblings, at http://charlieray45.wordpress.com. It's mainly a book review blog now, so you'll see what I'm reading, but I also put writing advice, WIP, and other writing and photography related stuff on it. If you'd like to get a look at all my books, check out my Amazon Author page at http://www.amazon.com/Charles-Ray/e/B006WMLEZK.

From the Chronicle of Pip of Pandara

Child of the Flame

Pip is a foundling, being raised by the tanner, Auric, and his wife, Ludmilla. Small for his age, Pip is the target of bullies in his home town, but when he's kidnapped trying to defend Queen Daphne, he discovers that he has in interesting, and powerful, heritage.

Pip's Revenge

After Pip rescues Queen Daphne, and she discovers that he's in fact her late sister's child, and heir to the throne of Pandara, she makes him head of the new Pandaran army. The tyrant who kidnapped Daphne is back, though, and Pip decides to rid the land of him once and for all.

Here, There Be Demons

Princess Miko of Alluria asks Queen Daphne for help to deal with a demon plaguing her land. Pip is sent on the mission, and learns that there is more to everything, and everyone, than meets the eye.

Charles Ray

Other books by this author:

Al Pennyback mysteries
Color Me Dead
Memorial to the Dead
Deadline
Dead, White, and Blue
A Good Day to Die
The Day the Music Died
Die, Sinner
Deadly Intentions
Death by Design
Till Death Do Us Part
Deadly Dose
Dead Man's Cove
Dead Men Don't Answer
Deadly Paradise
Kiss of Death
Death in White Satin
Death and Taxis
Deadbeat
A Deadly Wind Blows
Death Wish
Deadly Vendetta
A Time to Kill, A Time to Die

The Buffalo Soldier series:

Buffalo Soldier: Trial by Fire
Buffalo Soldier: Homecoming
Buffalo Soldier: Incident at Cactus Junction
Buffalo Soldier: Peacekeepers
Buffalo Soldier: Renegade
Buffalo Soldier: Escort Duty
Buffalo Soldier: Battle at Dead Man's Gulch
Buffalo Soldier: Yosemite
Buffalo Soldier: Comanchero
Buffalo Soldier: Range War
Buffalo Soldier: Mob Justice

Other fiction

Angel on His Shoulder
She's No Angel
Child of the Flame
Pip's Revenge
Here, There Be Demons
Wallace in Underland
Further Adventures of Wallace in Underland
Dead Letter and Other Tales
The White Dragons
The Dragon's Lair
Dragon Slayer
The Last Gunfighters
The Culling
*Frontier Justice: Bass Reeves, Deputy
    U.S. Marshal*

Angel on His Shoulder-Revised Edition
Battle at the Galactic Junkyard

Nonfiction
*Things I Learned from My Grandmother About
   Leadership and Life*
*Taking Charge: Effective Leadership for the
   Twenty-first Century*
Grab the Brass ring
*African Places: A Photographic Journey
   Through Zimbabwe and southern Africa*
A Portrait of Africa
There's Always a Plan B
*In the Line of Fire: American Diplomats in
   the Trenches*
Looking at Life Through My Lens

Children's books
The Yak and the Yeti
Samantha and the Bully
Molly Learns to Share
Where is Teddy?
Catie and Mister Hop-Hop

Charles Ray

About the Author

Charles Ray has been writing fiction since his teens. He won a Sunday school magazine writing contest when he was thirteen, and having his byline on a short story published in a national publication forever hooked him on writing. During his time in the army (1962-1982) he often moonlighted as a newspaper or magazine journalist, and was the editorial cartoonist for the Spring Lake (NC) News, a weekly newspaper, during the 1970s. In addition to his writing, he was an artist/cartoonist and photographer for a number of publications, including Ebony, Eagle and Swan, and Essence, and had a monthly cartoon feature and did several covers for Buffalo, a now-defunct magazine that was dedicated to showcasing the contributions of African-Americans to the country's military history.

After retiring from the army, he joined the U.S. Foreign Service, and served as a diplomat in posts in Asia and Africa until his retirement in 2012. He has worked and traveled throughout the world (Antarctica is the only continent he hasn't visited), and now, as a full time writer, continues to globetrot looking for interesting things to write about, draw, or take pictures of.

A native of Texas, he now calls Maryland

home. For more on his writing and other projects, check one of the following Web sites:

http://charlesaray.blogspot.com
http://charlieray45.wordpress.com
http://www.twitter.com/charlieray45
http://www.facebook.com/charlieray45
http://www.flickr.com/photos/charlesray45/
http://www.viewbug.com/member/charlesray

www.ingramcontent.com/pod-product-compliance
Lightning Source LLC
Chambersburg PA
CBHW071500170626
46811CB00007B/2651